SAVING SOPHIA

A HISTORICAL ROMANCE

JOHANA GARDENER

plicit Press

CHAPTER 1

SOPHIA'S MOTHER is bothered most by the awful inconvenience of it all. Mary has always thought her husband very prudent when it came to matters of travel, especially where these matters concerned their youngest. Rowan would always go to great pains to make sure that Sophia would travel safely and comfortably. But at his insistence, Sophia will be travelling to visit her cousins at the request of her uncle. And so Mary can do no more than to help her prepare for the visit.

She'll be sending Anne, Sophia's lady-in-waiting to help her on the journey, and also to attend to Sophia at her cousins. As they pack up what seems like too much for a visit meant to last no more than a month, Mary wonders about the mystery surrounding this visit. Rowan would normally show her the letter requesting Sophia's visit, but he's mislaid it. And he would never want Sophia to miss his birthday celebration, which is what is going to happen if Sophia takes this journey now.

"It's all just very strange Sophia, all of it!" Mary doesn't hide her anxiety from her youngest.

"I know mother. But he wouldn't insist I go if it wasn't important to him. Father must have a very good reason for wanting me there with such urgency." Sophia trusts her father blindly.

When her mother leaves the room Sophia throws herself onto her bed and lets out a very loud sigh. She knows that if her mother thought she was anxious that this would just perpetuate her mother's anxiety.

"Oh, Anne it is strange. Mother has no idea who these cousins are or this uncle. Father is very secretive about it all and we travel with barely a guard. It will be you and I, Ian, and Noah..." Sophia lets the sound of Noah's name hang in the air for a minute before bringing it to an end and closing her mouth.

"At least there's that, Noah..." Anne has known Sophia and cared for her long enough to know that this sentence will mean the same thing to them both. But it will remain as it has since forever, between them.

They finish packing just as the carriage pulls up to the front of the Manor. Noah and Ian, one of Rowan's most faithful guards, load the trunks.

"Where is father?" Sophia is anxious now because it seems that her father isn't going to see her before she goes. She moves through the house while everyone gathers by the carriage. Rowan is nowhere to be seen.

Rowan is in the chapel. On his knees, he moves his fingers over his rosary over and over again as he whispers fervent prayers. Mary finds him.

"Rowan, what is it? Who is this uncle? And these cousins? You're not sending Sophia to court Rowan are you?" Mary really just needs to be sure what she is sending her youngest to.

"Mary you worry. I would never burden Sophia with

the responsibility of the court, not with the way things are there. It's just safer for her to be visiting elsewhere, in case the king again sets his heart on her. I won't be able to discourage him again. We wouldn't want her to go the way of Anne Boleyn." Rowan tries to explain himself.

"That Boleyn girl was foolish, as were her parents. I want no part of court Rowan. This life is enough for me." Mary couldn't be more serious.

"And for me, wife. Now let's go and see our youngest off. The journey is long and they best be getting on." He leads his wife from the chapel and they find Sophia in the foyer.

Rowan throws his arms into the air as soon as his eyes have fallen on Sophia. Her arms too are open to receive and embrace her father, sending her on a strange journey to the far North to meet with these new cousins.

He says nothing to his daughter still that gives her any clue about where she is going or why. Mary is anxious too for this information but all Rowan does is weep, completely out of character for the nobleman, master of many lands, respected by great men, and often offered a place at court.

Mary and her twelve daughters, flanked by their husbands, all of the noble lineage, and their sons, no daughters, can only look on for as long as it takes for Rowan to finally release his thirteenth daughter, his youngest daughter, and allow her into the hands of Ian and Noah so that they may help her into the carriage. He taps the carriage with his staff after a word in Ian's ear and then turns into the house, leaving the others to watch as Sophia disappears down the gables that line the path to the magnificent residence that is Rowan Manor.

Mary doesn't know what to make of her husband's uncharacteristic emotion but chooses to distract herself with her many grandsons and her daughters she sees only twice a year now if she finds herself so fortunate.

"It must have to do with marriage, I suspect," Anne speaks boldly now that she feels she is out of earshot of Master Rowan. But she also speaks in whispers as though she can be heard outside the carriage.

"Oh don't be silly Anne, surely a suitor would have come calling at my father's house for my approval? Surely father and mother would not assume to make such an arrangement without my involvement, not for me, their youngest? And certainly not when it was not this way with my sisters?" Sophia is suddenly anxious, Anne has never been wrong, even in jest. Anne simply takes her hands over Sophia's, assuring her that whatever lies ahead, she is going to be with her.

They look out of the windows of the carriage, designed and built like all of Rowan's carriages for both comfort and safety. He insists on both when his daughters or his wife are required to travel. The day is warm but comfortable. They watch as her father's lands unfold in familiar patterns that let her know how far they've traveled. Sophia's chest heaves as far as her corset will allow.

The men sit side by side in silence. Ian is in control of the two steeds that pull them along. Noah is on hand to assist him with minor duties, and also to assist Sophia should anything arise along the way that might prove too much for Anne.

They could not be more different. Ian is cut from a warrior's cloth and is able to assess and assert any situation. He also has enough experience to carry them all safely through the woody route he has chosen to get them to their destination. Noah is uncertain of himself, growing up different and almost needy. Not that you would tell it looking at him now. Hard work has packed on everything a young man needs to make him attractive.

All familiarity is now gone, Sophia has no idea where she is. This is disconcerting since she's traveled from her home many times in every direction and always known what to expect along the way. But now they're surrounded by woods. Anne tries to reassure her that perhaps Ian is using a route through a part of the woods that hug the extreme left of her father's land to get them to their destination quicker. Perhaps he too is not up to six days of carriages and village inns or expecting hospitality along the way from nobles in her father's name.

Sophia needs confirmation. "Where are we Sir Ian?", she asks, leaning out of the window at an angle that has Anne grab onto her waist and half pull her back. Why she wouldn't slide open the flap that would send her voice directly out front to Ian is typical of Sophia's character.

"Just making speed Lady Sophia", Ian responds with authority. "Now get back inside before you toss us all onto the forest floor", he orders.

The forest suddenly opens and the trees let through all the might of the sun, still burning at remarkable strength even for the early afternoon. Anne uses the flap for the purpose for which it was designed and asks that her mistress be given rest. Sophia doesn't really need it but will feign fragility for the enjoyment of this beautiful, unfamiliar place she has never seen.

After the men have set up a canopy, the women enjoy a light tea. Noah and Ian enjoy what they have had packed for themselves. Still, they do not speak to each other, something that both women have noticed.

"It's unusual how little they say to one another", Anne offers.

"Perhaps it's the years between them or rank. Perhaps Noah is comfortable just following orders", Sophia speaks with authority about Noah, someone she has played with since childhood when they would swim with the other children with little concern of sex or covering more than what made them male or female.

They dismiss it as a matter between men and continue to enjoy their tea. Sophia stretches her eyes as far as she can and sees nothing that she has seen before. Again strange anxiety fills her, moving from her belly up into her chest and filling her head so that her face flushes. Anne fans her, knowing instinctively that her flustered look has nothing to do with the heat.

Noah remembers fondly their youth. Sophia was always far too nice to him than her position required, something the older girls cautioned her about often. But she was reckless and free-spirited and so he too dared to allow himself to proceed with their games with a measure of abandon. His mother would always punish him when news of him swimming half-naked with the young Lady Sophia got to her. Rowan would leave Sophia's punishment to her mother, a light reprimand behind closed doors which always ended in a giggle. Noah always bore a representation of his punishment when he jumped half-naked into the fountain with Sophia the very next day.

Ian watches Sophia, carefree but not. He thinks of the toll the journey ahead will take on her. But he has mapped out the best route to their destination, a destination even he would not have chosen for the young woman he's known practically all her life. She's called him Sir Ian long before even he was knighted and chose to stay in service to Rowan despite now having his own lands. He is sad. But years of fighting on the frontline of bloody battles make it impossible for this to surface enough so that it is detectable.

The men continue to watch Sophia, each for their own reasons. Sophia is oblivious to Ian, assuming that he is doing his job with great care out of love and respect for her father. She does catch Noah's eyes occasionally but doesn't hold his gaze long enough for her strange childhood friend to feel uncomfortable. She knows that he has always been shy; but not so much with her. Still, she gives him the space to search for what he thinks he might find upon her person, or within.

Ian is anxious to get back on the road so that they may pass the night with good food and warm beds. He knows this road. He has traveled it four times to ensure that he knows it very well. So he knows that if they don't move now they will not make the first hospitable village by nightfall, and be left to the mercy of the woods and the evil they conceal. It takes half the time it took the men to set up for them to back up and move along, the strong stallions at a light gallop.

There is an uncomfortable tension back at Rowan Manor. The master of the house paces the long halls of his home in silence, responding to all manner of questions with a nod or a slight shaking of his head. Everyone knows not what to make of this, not associating it immediately with Sophia's departure since she has traveled often on her own to visit relatives even as a child.

Most anxious is Mary. For the first time, she has no real detail about a trip she has been asked to send her youngest son. And then that she will stay for a month? She has no idea who these relatives are and why they suddenly want to meet her child. Why would they not make the trip and meet all her children, and in fact her? Why would Rowan not insist on this, so that he can show his family to these people he seems to trust so implicitly? This is all very uncharacteristic of a man who has had such a level head that he has extended his wealth over the years without having to accept an invitation to court, a man who has not a single unhappy laborer in his fields.

She follows him at a careful distance, giving him the space to process the many things that are fighting for attention in his head, but close enough to be on hand if he relents and decides to let her into what has him, and now the whole house unnerved. Even the grandchildren play in silence, unsure of this grandfather they don't recognize. But Rowan remains forthcoming with nothing.

"Is it Sophia, husband?" Mary will suffer his response for information about where her child will be in six days.

"Mary, let me be." He has dismissed her just once before in their marriage when he was hiding an injury after being thrown by a horse during a race with her brother. Fortunately, her brother was more forthcoming with the information needed for Mary to attend to her husband before infection made her a young, childless widow. She assumes that somehow, something has badly affected his pride. And again, he will not say what.

She reclines to her parlor and loses herself in embroidery she had spent many afternoons doing with Sophia. It would have been finished a long time ago had Sophia not enjoyed chatting with her mother about everything...Sophia!

At dinner, Rowan chooses to eat alone. His daughters, their husbands, and also their children are now expectedly uncomfortable in their father's house. Mary cannot convince them to stay as long as they've planned and they all resolve to leave in the morning in the hope that Mary will get to the bottom of it all. They will return in time for Rowan's birthday feast anyway. But their children are now incredibly anxious and so they choose to remove them from the situation.

Rowan doesn't even come out to say goodbye when he is told that all twelve of his daughters are leaving. All of his sons-in-law however bid him farewell, a few offering a measure of an explanation and promising to return with the grandchildren as soon as he is feeling better, perhaps when Sophia is back. Rowan cannot help but weep bitterly as soon as the last of them has left him.

Tears are evident on his face after hours of crying when Mary finds him in the garden under his favorite tree. She remembers how he used to play with Sophia like a little girl under this very tree and is suddenly overcome with a pang in the pit of her belly, the parts of herself that house a mother's instinct. She takes hold of Rowan from behind and gives his broad shoulders such a squeeze that he turns abruptly and steadies himself in expectation of an attack.

"Where have you sent my child Rowan?"

"Your child? Your child, Mary? I had no hand, no part in her making, in her upbringing, that you claim her for yourself with such vehement authority?"

"Where is Sophia, Rowan?"

Every question is left hanging in the summer air so that Mary turns into the house and Rowan loses himself down the path to the bottom of the garden that has on it all of Sophia's favorite things. This is typical of most arguments between the pair, one a man half Scot, half English blue-blood-albeit a light shade of blue-and a woman of rich noble French descent.

Mary knows from much experience, thirty years married to her husband that her answers won't come easily with her approach. She has to come to him differently, with a vulnerability that overshadows even her own, enough for him to feel that these answers will protect her from harm.

She sets about drawing him the kind of bath she would draw him in the early years. The very kind of bath that saw her pregnant for most of her marriage, give or take a year in between. The room smells of everything that made her husband relax, even after the most trying hunts; the very bath that saw her husband in bed with her with no appetite for dinner, or anything else. Rowan finds that she has even made his favorite kind of tea, chamomile and lavender infusion that he insisted every one of his daughters, and in case of an emergency, all of the kitchen maids, learn to make.

Without a word, Mary removes his outer garments. Rowan knows that to resist her after so much effort would greatly offend the French woman he has loved for as long as he has known of love. The French make it known, in love and war, just how easily they are offended. After much time he stands naked in front of his wife. Regular hunts with his knights and trying rides with his sons-in-law have kept him every bit as beautiful as she has known him. They have both aged very well, a consequence of both privilege and a very strong bloodline.

Only after he has settled comfortably in the large tub, a grand import from Paris, a wedding gift from Mary's favorite uncle, does she hand her husband his tea. She leaves him to enjoy it in silence, knowing that the distraction of her hands on him might be too much right now. She leaves him to his thoughts.

Rowan requests two more cups of tea before he is ready to fully indulge in the fragrant bath. Mary hopes that her efforts have softened his resolve to keep this demon that gnaws so fiercely at him from inside, within. Even when she takes a cloth to his broad, hairy back, there is no resistance, no objection. Still, no words have passed between them save Rowan's request for more tea.

But French women have a way with men. And Rowan is every part a man. But he is an Englishman, and this has proven most complicating at times. His responses are unpredictable and often what he does makes no sense. Still, she has succeeded with him almost as often as she has failed. So she continues, however cautiously.

She doesn't dress her husband for dinner, but for bed. Mary will serve his dinner in the bedroom, assuming that he will want to eat alone again. As she prepares his tray with the help of the kitchen staff she suppresses all the questions that her instincts need her to ask her husband. She tries to suppress all the scathing comments she urgently needs to make at him, the most pressing being that he could drive his children and grandchildren from his house, albeit by a shift in his demeanor.

Mary leaves her husband to eat, and she goes down to eat alone at her massive dining table. She looks at the many seats that sit empty and wonder how long it will be so. She hopes in silence that by tonight she will have made some progress. She eats quicker than she would if she'd had direct seated company and conversation at the table. Then she goes immediately to ready herself for bed.

When Rowan and Mary are in bed she moves up close to him from behind. She holds her husband and lets him feel her warmth. Nothing passes between them about Sophia. Mary reaches her arms around him and holds tightly onto his chest. Her hands move slowly down towards the parts of him she knows will open him up to answering her questions a little more honestly. Rowan takes hold of her hands and moves them back up to his chest. He settles back into her and falls asleep.

It is now a little darker than everyone in the wood is comfortable with. No sign of a village or an inn. And it's been a good while since Sophia last roughed it. She trusts that Noah and Ian will go out of their way to make her comfortable, but still, she'd rather be inside with a warm bed and a hot bath. The inside of the carriage fills with the same dark orange as the outside and Sophia can't help but look out of her window. The forest is drowning in the last light of sunset so that even the trees don't look much like trees. Sophia places her hand on the inside of the carriage where she knows just on the other side is Noah. Anne just smiles.

But then suddenly it is dark. And in the darkness, Ian has picked up his pace. It's clear that he too has no desire to spend the night outside. The women hold on, slightly anxious. Ian continues to pick up the pace.

"Perhaps we're close," Anne says, her panic clear on her face.

"Perhaps" Sophia is also visibly anxious.

Both women sit back in their seats, not wanting to make any sudden movements that might upset Ian and his plan. The carriage charges on through the woods. Sophia knows that something is wrong and she wants to ask Ian to stop. She will survive a night in the woods. She's done it before. And besides, Noah and Anne are with her. She tries to stand and reaches for the flap. But before she can flip it open the entire carriage lifts completely off of the ground and stays in the air for an unnatural length of time.

You hear nothing but horses. Anne doesn't scream. Sophia doesn't scream. The men are silent save for their instructions to the horses, instructions the horse cannot possibly carry out. The carriage continues to drag along the forest floor until eventually, the horse is silent. Then everything is silent. Sophia cannot bring herself to look up, or around.

Then the side door that is now above Sophia opens and the carriage fills with the beginnings of moonlight. Noah reaches his hand into the carriage and Sophia takes it. He helps her out. Then he checks on Anne. The news is not good. Sophia looks around for Ian and sees that Noah has covered him with his cloak. His face too is covered. Anne and Ian are dead. Sophia weeps, but only for a moment as she needs to take on the practicality required by this situation.

"Are you alright Sophia?" Noah asks at last. Still, he finds it difficult to speak with her casually in adulthood.

"I'm alright Noah thanks. Are you alright?" Sophia is remarkably composed.

"I am, we need to find anything that we can use for the trip back home." Noah is already rummaging through the contents of the baggage that is now all across the forest floor. He checks Ian for weapons. But instead of just a dagger and a sword, he finds a very interesting letter. He has no intention of letting Sophia see it, but it's too late. She is behind him. Sophia pulls the letter from him and walks away, taking the torch from Noah and reading it three times before the contents of it settle.

"So my father is sending me off to be married to a man I don't know for the sake of saving my family and my home?" Sophia drops to the ground in a heap and lets out a very big sigh.

CHAPTER 2

NOAH IMMEDIATELY STARTS to set up camp for the night. He gives Sophia the space she needs to try and process what she now knows. Noah notices that Sophia's discomfort seems to have less to do with more than the letter, which is in fact a contractual agreement. He goes into her and starts to examine her. He sees nothing obvious.

"What is it, Sophia?" Noah is genuinely concerned.

"I don't know; strange stabbing sensations." Sophia knows that Anne would know immediately what the problem was.

"Raise your arms, slowly." Noah is uncertain what he is looking for.

The pain intensifies and Sophia drops her hands. Noah sees what is wrong. The bones of her corset have come loose and are threatening to pierce through her in many places. Noah takes a dagger and carefully begins to slice the elaborate accessory off of Sophia. With a final snap of the blade, the entire contraption comes undone so that Sophia takes her hands to her chest and hugs herself. Noah gets her what she needs to cover up and to be both warm and comfortable.

Noah works quickly to get their camp set up. Sophia is warmed by a modest blaze, Noah nervous about drawing any unnecessary attention to them. They are both not hungry but force a tiny amount of broth from what they have salvaged, eating it in silence. Then Noah leaves Sophia and goes off to bury Anne and Ian. To his surprise, Sophia joins him, says a prayer, and then helps him fill in the graves. They mark them so that they can let their families know where they lie so that they can take them home later. The horses will have to make peace with this strange place being their final resting place.

They settle around the fire which is already threatening to burn into coals. There is nothing to say now. Tomorrow will have the necessary clarity for Sophia to make more sense of everything. She just wants to sleep now and mourn her lady-in-waiting alone. Noah is very good about people, and even when he hears her weep, often uncontrollably throughout the night, he knows that he just needs to leave her to her own processes.

"We should start heading back," Noah speaks as though there is no other possibility

"Back" Sophia wipes the sleep from her eyes, both she and Noah having woken just before dawn but feeling like they've slept forever and had every bad dream.

"Yes, back... surely now that you know you need to get to your mother and get her to convince your father to raise an army instead of just giving you away to someone you have never ever seen?" Noah cannot imagine that Mary had any part in this arrangement.

"Noah no, I can't. You didn't see my father before I left. Something about this person has struck every kind of fear into my father. He would not have sent me so easily if he

believed any sort of battle could be won. We must continue." Sophia is braver than Noah expected her to be.

"But only Ian knew where exactly we were going"
Noah can't imagine being the one to deliver Sophia.

"Yes, but it says his name here, so we can simply ask as
we go. John-Henry, Lord Baron; He doesn't even sound too
bad. I just cannot let them down. I will not fail my father,
not even in this." Noah knows that there is nothing more
to say.

They pack up only what they can comfortably carry.
Noah decides on where he thinks Ian was headed with
them. Sophia raises her hair into a high bun and lifts her
skirt to above her knees by rolling it repeatedly at the waist.
She looks less like a privileged lady and more like a milk-
maid. Noah keeps his giggles to himself.

They move steadily, with a little conversation to
conserve energy. The path isn't really even a path. It's a
seldom-used trail that cuts through the forest. They can't
even be sure that they aren't walking in the wrong direction.
But they will have an idea once they meet people who
know. If their memories serve them both well, there are
homesteads no more than half a day's walk in any direction
from her home.

Sophia feels the strain of the heat as it starts to establish
itself. The day will be very hot. Noah already feels sorry for
her and makes sure as much as he can to keep them under
the trees. The forest opens up almost as often as it shelters
them from the heat. Sophia appreciates this almost as much
as she would if Noah suggested they rest. But he doesn't.

Then his hand goes up into the air and Sophia stops. He
turns to her and puts his finger to his lips. But it's too late.
What he has just heard has heard them and seen them for
almost two hours. They get down on their knees and look

straight down at the ground. Noah whispers for Sophia not to look up at all. It could turn out okay for them if they did not make eye contact with these bandits who have managed to track them from the accident scene.

"So what have we here?" one of them steps forward and runs his hands over Sophia's face.

"Please, don't hurt her." Noah wants to get up and fight them but has no idea how many they are or what the contents are of their armory.

Both Noah and Sophia are stripped of the goods they carry and the bandits rummage through the loot. There is nothing of value, Sophia having decided to leave all her belongings back at the carriage. She has carried just one dress and some scents and oils so that she is a little more presentable when she meets her husband. It seems to go on forever, nobody speaking.

Then one of them discovers the letter. He reads it to himself and then passes it around.

"You'd do better to move in the opposite direction squire, take the young miss with you, set up home at the bottom of a hill. It would be more humane to leave her to the beasts in the forest than to take her to the Blood Baron." There is a softer, sympathetic tone in the bandit's voice, and both Noah and Sophia lookup.

"You know him?" Sophia asks.

"Everyone knows him, or of him." His reply sounds every bit like the warning it is.

The bandits don't waste too much time with them, repeating their caution that it would be better for them to go in another direction. They leave Sophia with the chain around her neck and the three rings on her fingers. Enough loot has been gathered from the carriage. Noah watches as they ride off and looks at Sophia, hoping that some sense has found its way into her now. They have however helped themselves to Ian's sword and his dagger.

"No, we must go on. At least we know that we are moving in the right direction." Sophia tries to sound firm so that Noah knows she will not negotiate.

"But we also have confirmation of his character. Surely this must move you to reconsider. Perhaps we should just vanish. I can hide you, protect you. I can keep you." Noah doesn't really know what he is saying.

"For how long, Noah; and what happens to my family when I don't arrive?" Sophia is more practical than Noah would like her to be.

More silence now as they keep in the same general direction. Noah allows himself to imagine all the things he had secretly longed for when he was old enough to no longer be comfortable in front of Sophia. He remembers how he watched her grow, and how he would tell his mother of all the changes he had noticed in Sophia on any particular day. His mother had always reprimanded him, reminding him of their station in the house that took them in when they had nowhere to go. Noah was only three at the time.

Sophia too wonders about her childhood. She remembers all the plans she and Anne had, all the dreams and fantasies of who her husband would be. She imagined how, like her sisters, she too would have an army of sons, pleasing her husband and her father. It was a beautiful fantasy. They often shared these with her mother. Mary would just look at her youngest fondly and shake her head, knowing that nothing was impossible for her; nothing was out of her reach.

The letter too consumes them. They have their own idea of what went on in Rowan's head when he agreed to this. It must have been torture. He must have labored over it for a long time. Or had he? Sophia thinks he must have. She knows he must have. Noah can't imagine doing the same. He can't imagine the sacrifice. But he has never been in such a situation and so he stops himself immediately from judging Rowan, who had always been so good to his mother and him.

The sun hangs high in the sky now and the sweat falls from both of them. A tree casts a massive shadow just a little ways off and Sophia makes for it. She can't help it. She needs to stop. Noah doesn't even question her, any delay in getting to their destination is most welcome. He checks Ian's money bag. Rowan definitely wanted his daughter to have a very comfortable trip.

The earth is cool where the sun cannot reach it. They both sit leaning up against the tree and pass a water skin between them. It will need to be filled soon. Noah looks at Sophia with a new curiosity. He remembers her helping with the burials. He remembers her rolling her skirt up, ready to get on with it. Who has Sophia actually become in plain sight? She seems remarkably capable. Her mother would definitely not approve.

He thinks of everything he knows about Rowan. He has an army of knights. Noah doesn't know how many. He has an entire land filled with men and even women who love him enough to go to arms for him if needed. Rowan has been invited to court many times; the king has visited him often, so surely he could call on some sort of support. But the court is a strange thing. And unless you're in it, you are most definitely out. So while you have the king's favor, you do not have his full protection.

Why would Rowan not even make an effort? Probably the timing of it all. It could take longer for him to rally support for himself than it would for the Blood Baron to descend upon them with his armies. And who knows how many make up this army. It truly must have been a very difficult decision to make. There must really have seemed to be no other option. And with England still so vast, spread out over incredible distances, it was days, months even, between the many noble estates.

Noah makes a full and firm commitment to not even try to put himself in Rowan's shoes. He has made an incredible sacrifice. All he can do now is help Rowan see it through and hope that Sophia will be treated as her upbringing has made her accustomed to. He repacks their loads so that again they are easy to carry. There is no food and it is time to get to a village or an inn. This journey was going to be hard on Sophia in the carriage already. But now that she has to walk, it will be near unbearable. Noah resolves to get them a pair of horses just as soon as he can and shakes his head, admiring her reliance and the fact that not once has she complained or thrown any sort of tantrum.

When night falls and there is still no sign of a village, Noah snares them two rabbits and some quails. Sophia prepares them quickly and they eat them hungrily. They cool down in turn in a pond they almost missed and then dry up by the fire that cooked their dinner. It will be another night under the stars. Sophia is the one who now goes to great lengths to prepare comfortable beds for them both.

Sleep comes quickly, even for Noah. Sophia's head fills with dreams of home. She dreams that she has listened to Noah and that they have made their way back toward her father's house. She sees all the familiar fields that she has played in so often throughout her life. The workers tilling the land, the children playing, the animals grazing; it's all just so perfect.

Over and over her chest fills with the anxiety she knows her father will feel when he sees her. She knows that he will know that she knows where he has sent her. He will have no words for her. She knows that there will be tears. And there will also be an almost absoluteness about the fate of all her father's people.

Her mother will know nothing. She will be sad about the accident but happy that her child is alive. There will be a celebration. There will be an interesting cloud of joy mixed with ominous doom. It will hang heavy and smiles will not last longer than needed. Sophia shakes herself from the dream, hating that she is conflicted now about saving her family.

There really isn't a choice. She must just do what needs to be done. There are worse things that she could be subjected to. And for the most part, she doesn't really know for sure what it is she is going to do. She looks over to where Noah is sleeping, anxiety etched across his forehead like a family of streams. She haggles back down and tries to go to sleep.

Again sleep comes easy. But her dream remains the same. That she would not sacrifice herself for her family would not make her Rowan's daughter. She will do what needs to be done and it will be over. Everything becomes normal after a while anyway. She will wait for things to become normal. And she will embrace this normal.

Noah sleeps through the night while Sophia's night is restless. The morning finds her standing a little way off and staring over the nothing in front of her. This journey has them a day's journey on foot plus half a day, maybe less by carriage from her father's house. Noah ponders this as he watches Sophia. He makes a decision that he knows will probably not sit well with the lady once she figures out his rouse.

For one to take a decision in defiance not only of his charge but also of his master is punishable by death. But Rowan has never executed a man. And Noah has convinced himself that he can talk Rowan into taking up an army and fighting for his lands and the happiness of his daughter. Noah will do anything for Sophia's happiness.

Breakfast is quail eggs. It's a fortunate morning and they find dozens, saving what they don't eat for later. The conversation is light and not about where they are headed. Noah doesn't know exactly how to turn them around without making it obvious. But then he realizes that Sophia too has never been in this part of the forest and so everything looks to her like everything else. He suggests that they find a shady place to rest for the warmest part of the day, and travel at night when it's cooler and safer.

By nightfall, Sophia appreciates his suggestion. They move faster and don't need to rest as much. There is also no need to drink as much water. Noah takes Sophia by the hand and guides her through the forest. Often he moves them through the shallows of the streams and rivers that they encounter. Then when he finds a part of a river that is shallow enough to cross completely he does. Sophia moves with him like a dancer, letting him lead her where he will in the pitch-black night.

They cross back and forward over streams and rivers so often that by the time they are moving in what Noah hopes is the right direction, the direction to Rowan's house, Sophia doesn't have a clue. Everything just seems to be moving forward at a respectable pace. The stars are seldom visible and there is ominous darkness, a cloud that hangs over them. Noah appreciates this because it has made it possible to fool Sophia. She will forgive him. She will understand.

Fortunately, they pass the shallow graves and what is left of the carriage at some point in the night. And only Noah sees them. He moves Sophia a little further away from them and tries for her to pick up her pace, excited that he is definitely on the right path. Eventually, just before dawn, they come off the path that Ian had deviated onto and are again on a familiar path on the outskirts of her father's property. Noah insists that they rest now.

Sophia sleeps easily; Noah not so much. He knows that when she opens her eyes she will know exactly where she is. Still, he rests up for the confrontation. It takes long enough but Noah eventually falls asleep and the morning sun gently kisses their sleeping faces as they dream of absolutely nothing. But sleeping doesn't last very long.

Sophia shakes Noah from his sleep. Her face is frantic.

"What have you done? How could you do this?" She slaps him across the face repeatedly. He lets her.

"We are going to figure it out when we are back in your father's house. We will tell them there was an accident. There was an accident Sophia. This is the truth. Your father will not think it strange that we returned." Noah now holds her hands, his face throbbing and red.

"But we know what this means. If we didn't then maybe, yes. But we know what this means. How will he make it work now? What will happen now?" Sophia struggles to get her hands free.

"We will figure it out. With your father, we will figure it out." Noah lets her hands go.

She gives it up. They are so close now that there really is no other option. They don't rest, moving in the familiar direction of everything they know. But the closer they get to her father's house, the more anxious Sophia gets. She cannot bring herself to speak another word to Noah. He will deal with her anger later. She will be sure of it. He will know just how angry she is at being made to look a fool. Not with all her education and wit.

Sophia takes the money bag from him and turns into a local seamstress. She has a laborers' dress with a massive bonnet made for her so that she is not recognizable. The last thing she needs now is for news of their return to get to her father before she does. The fields become increasingly richer. The sound of children laughing is everywhere. Old men gather around tiny stalls and play ancient games. Women help each other with quilts and other preparations for the winter. It's too early but everything else is already done and the harvest will come in earlier this year. And what a harvest it will be.

Rowan's house appears in the distance. Sophia stops and looks around her. Everything is just so perfect. Everyone is just so happy. She moves into the orchards at the bottom of her father's land where she played often, and still comes to think. Noah is now the one following. She sits under the trees that will only bear fruit in the winter. But still, the entire field smells of citrus and orange blossom. She lies on the floor with her face hidden in her hands.

What will she say to her father when she sees them? Noah has a good enough approach, but only if they didn't know the truth. So now they will again have to put up a rouse and pretend to know nothing about the letter, hoping that Rowan will see reason and make another plan. Maybe Rowan will take his daughter into his confidence. Everything just seems to hang in the air like the clouds. There just seems to be no real solution forthcoming.

"Sophia it's going to be okay." Noah doesn't know what else to say.

"No Noah, it isn't. Nothing is ever going to be okay again." She gets off the ground and starts to move through the orchard towards her father's house. She can feel nothing but the rapid beating of her heart, free to move in the absence of a corset. Noah just moves behind her, afraid to further aggravate the lioness. Sophia becomes less and less resolved though the closer they get to Rowan Manor.

There are people preparing the trees. Nobody really pays them much mind, recognizing Noah and so not worrying about who he is with. Sophia listens to how they appreciate their lives, their master. Nothing could be more perfect. Life has never been so full of promise. Their children are healthy and grow up well. Everyone is happy.

Sophia says nothing. She turns to face Noah and takes him by the arm. She moves him back in the direction that they came from. He just looks at her and lets himself be led. They get to the bottom of the orchard again and sit under the same tree.

"I can't do this. I demand that you take me to where my father intended. You will have all the money in this bag, what's left of it upon our journey's end, as compensation for your inconvenience." Sophia speaks with authority so that Noah can only nod.

So once again they are moving away from home, and away from safety. But nothing is safe here now. And they are really going to need to pick it up considerably if they are to avoid a misunderstanding because of Sophia's late arrival. This is serious business. Too much is at stake. Sophia has already had such a fantastic life. She can do this one thing for her parents. She must do this one thing for her father.

She loves that she has Noah mute. If they are not

speaking to each other then they move faster. They need to move as far away from here now as quickly as possible. And then figure out the rest of the journey. It won't be hard. Sophia believes that that will in fact be the easy part. But the sun will make it difficult. And already she has been tried immensely. Nothing in her life could have prepared her for this. But life will often serve you up what you least expect.

The sun moves high up in the sky and they both want to stop. They don't. For as long as they can, they stay under the trees and close to the streams. Sophia again has her skirt rolled up and her bonnet hangs loosely down her back. She recognizes where Ian had made his deviation, and so she does the same. Noah is impressed with her recollection. She would make an excellent tracker.

By the time the sun sets they are a day from the accident. Having made such excellent progress, they cannot continue. Dried meats purchased along the way will be their dinner. Sophia even insisted on some light ale. There is no need for a fire and so they simply get comfortable in their makeshift beds and let their thoughts move with them to slumber.

CHAPTER 3

IAN HAD OBVIOUSLY PLANNED to keep them on the side roads and so that is where they stay. The only concern they have now is that they might run into bandits who won't be as accommodating as the band they encountered the first time. Moving slowly during the day and then resting when the sun is at its most attacking is a strategy that works well for them. They then manage to move faster at the night, when it is cooler and everything seems more supportive of their journey. God will need to really be with them, all the way and beyond.

When the road disappears they take calculated guesses. It becomes more and more disturbing that they are making no contact with other people. There are just no homesteads or villages. How is it that this desolation, albeit plush and green, can exist so close to her home? It seems so incredibly out of place. But at least the night hides the awkward absence of people.

Noah cannot continue to let Sophia lead them on this journey. He needs a proper strategy that will provide both safety and swift passage. He slowly starts to take over the reins. And Sophia is so tired now that she simply lets him. He is soon leading them further and further from their home along roads that are both intriguing and unfamiliar. They open up carelessly so that you can't resist taking the next bend, just to see what it is you might find.

It's an incredible part of England. There is not a trace of the madness that is London, where executions have become a noble fetish. Even the peasants have developed a fondness for the smell of burning flesh, or the sounds of the guillotine. The drop and snap of a hanging excite even children in the street. There is nothing pleasant about London at the moment.

Out here England makes sense. Silence and calm that stretches as far as the eye can see with not an inkling that it will change at any time. You simply expect it to always be this way. Sophia imagines that this is how it will be in her new home. She imagines a haven away from the dramas of court with a man who wants nothing more than a young wife who will bear him an heir. John-Henry must know of her sisters and their reliable wombs. This is why she is the chosen one. But what if she is not like her sister?

"We're really getting a long way from home." Noah says with a heavy heart.

"I'm getting closer and closer to home." Sophia starts to settle into her new reality.

The landscape changes again as the night approaches. It's time to eat. They've not thought of this during the day, both consumed with reveries of home. But Noah will get to go back. Without Sophia, this is less than appealing, even with his mother at Rowan Manor. He will go back for her and move on with his life. He imagines that things will be strained between himself and Rowan. They will be strained for a very long time.

It is easy to miss what you don't know. But when you know a life intimately, the missing becomes an intense pain. It is this pain that Sophia tries to wash off of her while Noah finds a meal. But no matter how hard she scrubs, it just won't go away. She watches from inside the pond as Noah lights a fire and starts with dinner, rabbit from the smell of it.

By the time she is standing beside him, the rabbits are ready. Noah throws himself under the water and then makes a very quick exit. He is dripping wet when he grabs his supper and starts to pull it apart with his teeth. They both had no idea just how hungry they really were. They also have no clue just how tired they are. They have not slept in proper beds since they left Rowan Manor. And it has been a while.

The earth is soft though and so sleep is not uncomfortable. Sophia has really mastered the art of the outdoor bed. Noah admires her in silence. They lie under the stars and watch the world go by. Full bellies are a sure way to a good night's sleep. There is a calmness in the air that has them create for themselves the dreams they wish to have. And they stay within these dreams for as long as it takes for the night to become day. Again they wake up completely refreshed and rested.

The day is mildly hot. The heat is accompanied by a persistent drizzle. It is most welcomed and Sophia half dances in it. They walk through fields now, with no paths or roads in sight. It is cool and every kind of pleasant. Occasionally they throw themselves in the grass and let the rain wash over them. For the first time, there is a sound that isn't coming from them. It is so conspicuous because they have had nothing but nature and themselves for a while now.

Noah tries to make out what it is. As hard as Sophia tries she has no idea.

"Wait for her, stay low." He instructs her. Then he disappears into the tall grass towards the sound. It becomes a lively noise, not at all menacing as he had first thought. He moves on closer and closer, steadily making his way to the roaring laughter and the clanging of pints. People at last. A village! They will be able to rest up properly, and maybe even get themselves a pair of horses. Then the grass opens up and reveals a massive carnival ground. It's a traveling fare, massive, and really well supported. Noah looks around for the village but sees nothing. That's okay for now. He goes to get Sophia.

They try to make their baggage as compact as possible and then make for the fare. The first stop is the food stalls. Rich hearty black pudding and other things that cannot be found in the forest and they eat. There are cakes too and fresh juices. This is an incredible celebration, seemingly just because. Then they get themselves bags of sweets and other childish delights and make their way through the stalls to see what they can pick up that could make their trip more comfortable.

"We must let one of the villagers show us where their village is." Noah is planning the rest of the day.

"All we have to do is follow them when they start to leave. Now relax and have some fun." Sophia lets her hair down, literally.

"Only if you will, my Lady" Noah winks at her.

They move through the fare, mostly finding themselves in queues with children, playing the easier and more fun games. Noah wins a little too much and gives his winnings away to the children surrounding them with anticipation dripping from their eyes. The afternoon becomes evening before either of them has noticed and they are again eating. Chunks of beef that seem to have been cut for men disappear before them as they take in the flavors and the absolute indulgence of it all.

It's midnight when it all starts to come down and the villagers start to leave while the carnival hands get on with their work. Everything will be packed up and a smaller night festival, made up mostly of drinking really, will be set up in town. Noah and Sophia slip into the crowd and move with them as they make for home.

They have both not heard of the village before. It's not just one village, but a collection. People fall into the night and lose themselves as they are not sure if they want to go home. There are only thoughts of meat and bakes and ale. Noah immediately starts to look around for an inn. He asks anyone who doesn't seem too intoxicated. Eventually, he is directed to the only inn in the village. It really is a perfect fit for this village.

There is only one room left. They take it. It's a modest lodging. The bed is not as small as they expected. There is a basin in the corner for washing up, but no bath. Two blankets are on the bed but they are both unnecessary despite the rain coming down a little harder outside now. Noah and Sophia jump onto the bed, literally.

"This is nice," Noah says.

"Really?" Sophia bursts out laughing.

They lie next to each other and appreciate the mattress. It really feels like heaven. The bed seems like it was taken from Rowan's house and placed in this inn by magic. It fits them and they almost sink into it. This moves them closer to each other and they are almost rolling with laughter. Everything feels like their childhood.

"Everyone seems so happy." Sophia almost sighs as she says so.

"It's all thanks to your father. The further we get from his lands it will be very, very different." Noah knows this for sure.

"I know. And we're going to make sure that it stays that way."

The conversation drifts off and soon enough Sophia is asleep. She moves in towards Noah so that the only thing he can do is to hold her. Noah watches her face as it softens the deeper she goes into dreamland. He pulls a blanket over them without letting her slip from his arm. She really is being incredibly brave. Noah can't imagine how someone with her upbringing could have the courage to make such a life-altering decision.

Rowan has really built what can only be described as a happy kingdom. Where most of the population of England is hungry, the peasants miserable and mistreated, everyone who has a piece of land under Rowan, and even those who just work on Rowan's lands, they are all incredibly content. Happiness is a defined way of life.

Noah looks at Sophia and really understands what is driving her. She has her father's heart. People are more important than anything. People's happiness is extremely important to them. He lets his fingers hang just above her face, unable to bring himself to actually touch her. He really wants to touch her badly. But that would be most inappropriate.

He keeps Sophia in the comfortable cocoon created by his arms. But he is careful to move the parts of himself away from her that would give away the thoughts in his head. He tries as best he can to make himself comfortable enough to fall asleep. It doesn't happen. So eventually he frees Sophia from his arms and finds the letter in his bag. He reads it quietly. Then he reads it a little louder, not wanting to wake Sophia but wanting to hear the words in his ears.

Every time he reads it, it sounds differently. Sometimes it sounds formal, too formal, as though an entire series of discussions between all concerned led to the decision. Then it just sounds evil and twisted, the outcome of a negotiation between two evil men. Then he reads it again. And every word becomes a craftily created commitment of one who had no idea that these words are even being penned. It's an incredible document that seems to evolve all on its own. But no matter how it reads, the outcome remains the same.

Noah gets back into bed. He will need to be rested tomorrow for the journey ahead. They've already lost a substantial amount of time. For them to lose anymore could be a disaster. He takes the second blanket and throws it over himself. Noah tries to empty his mind enough to fall asleep. It doesn't come easily, but eventually, Noah is snoring, sleeping deeper than he has in weeks.

The sun doesn't shine directly into the room, allowing them to choose when to wake. But Noah has such a rigid sleep pattern that even though the room is still dark thanks to the heavy covering over the windows, he is awake just about as soon as the sun has come up. He feels completely rejuvenated. The covering over the windows also means that the room remains wonderfully cool. Noah takes a look outside and sees that life has already started on the streets below.

Returning the cover so that again the room is dark, he prepares a bath for himself. He sets it up in a far corner of the room, hoping to be done before Sophia wakes. But she seems to still be fast asleep. There is no need for warm water. The cool water is comfortable enough for him to have a decent wash. He is very anxious though that Sophia is right here in the room.

He removes his shirt and his trousers, covering himself from the waist down with a sheet. He takes a washcloth and works it over his head first, wetting his hair and then washing his face. Then he moves over his chest and up and down his arms. He has incredible arms. The entire right side of Noah's torso is wrapped in the most elaborate birthmark. It's a deep etching of the most incredible purple that fills half of his chest and goes halfway around his back.

It has often been mistaken for an infection or a burn. But even when Noah's mother explained this to the other children's parents they refused to play with him. She couldn't really blame them, and Noah never did. It is quite a disturbing thing to see. But really once you get used to it, it actually adds to everything else that makes Noah so incredibly attractive. He reaches quickly under the sheet with his washcloth and cleans his manhood and his legs. He watches Sophia the whole time.

What he doesn't know is that Sophia is very much awake. She has been watching him for a while. But it would be incredibly awkward for her to be awake while he is busy with his matters of personal hygiene. So she pretends to still be lost in sleep so that he can comfortably finish up. Noah goes through the awkward process of getting his pants on without removing the sheet. It takes a lot of skill but he gets it done. Then he lets the sheet fall to the ground. He puts on his socks and boots next, still throwing his eyes to the bed occasionally.

Still, he hasn't noticed that Sophia is awake. And she goes through almost uncomfortable lengths to make sure he doesn't. Sometimes she has to hold her breath, which just makes her want to laugh. So she exhales quietly out of her

mouth. She can't stop herself from watching him. Sophia
sees both the man that Noah is now and also the child that
he was when he arrived at her home. It was very exciting
and curious for everyone, this woman and her boy who just
turned up in the middle of a rainy night and asked for a
warm place for one night.

She remembers the look on Noah's face, the confusion
in his eyes, even though she too was just three. And the
thing that disturbed her most was his mother. This is why
she has not been able to lose this memory. She looked scared
and out of place in herself so what she was saying with her
mouth did not match her body. Sophia remembers her own
mother embracing this woman as though she understood
everything that she wasn't saying.

They let Noah play with them much later when they
were around five or six. It was a particularly hot summer.
Mary had allowed the children to play in the fountain in the
back garden, and when she caught Noah standing in the
distance watching, she urged him to join in. Sophia had
some of her cousins visiting, and those of her sisters young
enough for careless child's play were with them also.

Noah approached them cautiously. The other boys
already had their shirts off and were lost under the water.
The girls in their light summer dresses were bobbing up and
down. Noah's mother saw him going toward the others and
imagined that any time now he would be encouraged to take
his top off. She knew what this would mean. She tries to get
to them but Mary is already helping him out of his top. As
Mary throws it on the grass Noah wraps his arms around
himself.

Mary gives him a hug and tells him that it's okay to be
different. She tells the youngster that birthmarks make
people interesting and that he makes him more interesting

than most. She takes him by the hand and walks him to the other children. They stop swimming and jump out of the fountain, frightened visibly by his birthmark.

"This is Noah everyone, girls you know Noah. He's going to swim with you today." Mary introduces him.

There are immediate objections. Everyone is quick to point out his birthmark in the casual way that children have of stating the obvious. Noah's mother finally gets down to where they are and tries to take her son from Mary, needing to protect him from ridicule. But Mary lifts Noah up into her arms.

"This is Noah's mom. She can tell you how Noah got such an interesting birthmark." Mary is a very experienced mother.

"His father was a very powerful man from a very far-off land. And he was born with a birthmark just like Noah's. He was very determined to have a boy and every day he would think about it no matter where he was or what he was doing. Eventually, he became completely obsessed with having a little boy and it totally consumed his life.

So when he eventually found out that I was going to have a baby he prepared everything as though it could only be a boy. Everybody thought that he had lost his mind, and his subjects often laughed at him behind his back. Nobody could understand how he thought that he was suddenly able to predict the future. But he was convinced and there was no changing his mind.

The nine months that Noah was in my belly were some of the happiest. He was a calm baby and most of us, even the midwives, were convinced I was going to be having a girl. But we would not dare say this to Noah's father. So we let him believe what he did and the rest of us went with what years and years of experience said.

But the closer we came to knowing what was growing inside of me, I became more and more anxious. Noah's father became more and more excited. I was worried that when he found that it had been a girl all along he would be very angry. And he was such an unpredictable man that he was capable of absolutely anything. So I also started to pray that it would miraculously be a boy.

On the day of Noah's birth, it rained wildly. It was not possible for anyone to leave the house or for anyone to risk coming to the house. Fortunately, everything and everyone that we needed was already with us. And so there was no delaying his introduction to the world. I was prepared and the process started.

He was a very feisty chap. He was a fighter. It took forever to get him out, almost as though he was still very happy exactly where he was and wanted to be there a little bit longer. But I needed to put myself out of my misery, his father too. And with all the strength in me, I gave Noah to the world.

You can imagine everyone's surprise when in fact he actually was a boy. His father was beside himself and ran into the room immediately. He wanted to take the boy from the nurses but they wouldn't let him. It was just too soon. They gave him a clean swaddling cloth and then wrapped him up warmly. Finally, they handed him to me and he eventually stopped crying as I gave him his first feed.

Then his father came to see him when he was settled enough. He lifts him in the air and gently unwraps him, needing to see for sure that he has a son. He lets out a roar as his eyes fell between the little one's legs. He lifts him higher so that the light catches every part of him, and then we both noticed it. Noah had exactly the same birthmark, in exactly the same color as his father. There was absolutely nothing different about the birthmarks; we compared them very closely, fascinated. Noah's father was the happiest man on earth, and Noah was destined to be as great a ruler as he."

They are not sure if the story has done its work, but Sophia eventually jumps off the side of the fountain, grabs him by the hand and they both throw themselves into the water. Everybody else decides that they would suddenly rather play on the grass.

Once Noah has put his shirt on, Sophia opens her eyes. She stretches her arms above the covers so that he knows she is awake now. She has a strange smile on her face and Noah feels exposed. But he dismisses the feeling.

"Good morning. Did you sleep well?" Noah is nonchalant.

"Very, thanks. And you?" Sophia's voice is heavy with sleep.

"I did. But I can't help getting up at the same time each day. The routine is etched into my body and my mind. You're going to need to bathe. Would you like me to organize you some hot water?"

"No thank you, that won't be necessary. I'm going to be okay with what's in here." Sophia is out of bed now.

"Okay, I'm going to leave you then. Let me see what I can do about horses." Noah leaves the room.

He moves through the village trying to find anyone who actually has horses for sale. But nobody is willing to part with their horses with the harvest coming. He tries to negotiate with everyone who doesn't own a field or work on one, but even they lease their horses out during the harvest. It's proving a difficult task, no matter the price he offers.

Then he remembers the horses at the back of the inn. While he was reading the letter in the middle of the night he remembers hearing them. He looked out of the appropriate window and saw stables. It sounded like there were quite a few of them but he couldn't be sure. He makes his way back to the inn and finds the innkeeper.

"I need to make you an offer for two of your horses, solid ones able to take on a long journey with a light load." Noah gets straight to the point.

"Me horses aren't for sale lad." The innkeeper looks confused, wondering where this young man could have possibly got the idea that he was selling anything more than rooms.

But Noah is not a man that gives up easily, despite his weak negotiating skills. And soon enough he has the innkeeper showing him the better horses for long-distance travel. He picks two that seem capable of getting them there, not wanting to push his luck by picking the best ones. He saddles them up and they take them to the local blacksmith to be fitted with new shoes. They seem a happy enough pair of steeds and Noah takes them back to the inn. Sophia is absolutely thrilled and throws her arms around Noah, kissing her gratitude onto the side of his face.

CHAPTER 4

ROWAN MANOR IS SOMBER. Nobody has any idea about the dark cloud hanging over them that has been there since Sophia left. There are many rumors now. Everyone is whispering in the kitchens and the attic. Some save their whispers for the back courtyard by the safety of the washing lines. Others are brave enough to whisper in the hallways. But it's all just mad, horrible speculation. And all of it is wrong.

Mary is trying not to assume anything. She keeps running her house as smoothly as she always had. And with her husband's birthday coming up, she at least has something significant to distract her. She starts with the plans for the feast, albeit a little too early. She only allows herself to feel the fullness of her pain and anxiety in her private moments, by herself.

Another woman is also anxious about her own child. Noah's mother moves through her duties, mending and maintaining the massive drapes and tons of linen in the massive house. But her heart beats a continuously unsettled beat every time she thinks of her son. He is on a journey from the house that they have said will be more than two months at most. It seems to be taking forever to her although it has hardly been a month.

The staff feels the absence of Lady Sophia, and also the constant laughter and almost childish manner of Anne, her lady-in-waiting. The house is less happy. And nobody has any idea how to bring it to life. All they can do is their jobs. And then go to bed. It is well and truly a miserable situation. And everyone, absolutely everyone, is having a most terrible time.

Rowan's general responses are still just nods, accompanied by the occasional grunt. He moves through the halls looking at every picture of every member of his family. He spends far too much time in the garden alone. He eats alone more often than he eats with his wife. Mary has quite almost completely forgotten what her husband's voice sounds like. And even sadder, she has almost completely forgotten his touch.

But she carries herself with the airs of her station. Not once does her posture fall. Not once does her appearance betray the pain and anxiety inside her. Not once does she give in to her confrontational character and attack her husband, encouraging everyone to just be supportive until he is feeling better.

Despite her extraordinary composure, Rowan knows his wife. He knows that she needs something from him that will make her feel that he is on the road to recovery. He needs to try for some parts of his old self so that Mary sees that all is not lost and that everything is not as bad or as serious as they've all assumed. So he starts to prepare himself mentally and physically to be his old self, even just for a little while.

He starts by having every meal with her. She is taken

aback but still maintains her own position. He is clearly starting to come to her and she knows that this is no time to rush him. She might just set him back. There is light conversation and even some laughter. Once he even mentions Sophia and Mary has every hope that it won't be long before he reveals the truth about her.

"You know Mary, one day Sophia too will leave this house forever." He looks into the distance as he says it.

"I know Rowan. Our children have grown up well. But they have all grown up too quickly. We do see them whenever it is possible, the grandchildren too. So it really isn't that bad." Mary wonders if this is her husband's explanation for his behavior since Sophia's departure. It just seems too exaggerated.

But still, Rowan tries to behave normally. He goes riding again and takes his hunting team into the woods. They have good hunts, and when the hunts are bad, he accepts it casually. There is a relaxed demeanor about him that strangely enough doesn't seem contrived, even though it is. But Rowan really is doing it all from a place of love, so that it adds a level of sincerity to all his actions.

Everyone is easier around him now. Mary too becomes more and more receptive to this change, dropping her own guard. She will see what to make of this with the passing of time. There is no need at this moment to upset the applecart. Everyone has breathed a collective sigh of relief and it seems unnecessary to do anything that will simply make them all anxious again. She is as loving as she has ever been toward her husband and attentive to all his needs.

One night a long-missing need is suddenly in their bedroom. Rowan watches his wife preparing herself for bed. He too prepares himself, but to Mary's surprise he takes off all of his clothing and doesn't put on his sleeping robes. He jumps into bed naked, gets under the covers, and continues to watch her. She starts to feel awkward and uncomfortable, something she has not felt with him since the first few times they made love.

He gestures for her to come to him. She smiles shyly, not knowing what to do. This is the last thing that she has expected. But it was happening. And so she puts her brush on her dresser and goes to her husband. She removes her robe and jumps into bed with just her nightdress. Rowan pulls her to him and places his lips on hers. Mary moans, shivering at her husband's touch. This is most welcome, but she suddenly has no response for him.

Rowan can sense her confusion and so he knows that talking won't do. He guides her gently down the road he wants her to travel with him without saying a word. He proceeds to make love to her as gently as he ever has. There is nothing wrong with the intimacy between them. Their bodies know each other so well that they seem to work with little input from the owners. Mary is glad for this reflex because of her own accord, she would have been at a dead end.

Rowan makes a very intimate effort to please his wife. They make love for most of the night until both of them fall into a love drunk slumber. It was good, but a little unfamiliar for Mary. She can't quite place her finger on it but when she wakes up she feels like her husband was simply trying too hard. This is something that he has never had to do before. She is even less convinced now of this change in Rowan's behavior. But everyone is happy so she says nothing.

Things continue to seemingly improve and the preparations for the birthday become an actual formal scheduled event now in the house. Rosters are set up and what can be prepared so far in advance is prepared. What needs to be ordered from elsewhere and everything that needs to be fetched is. Some of the birthday supplies need to be fetched from as far as London. Rowan has suddenly got very extravagant tastes and wants an extremely extravagant party to match.

Noah and Sophia are again under the stars. It really no longer bothers them and they know that they will probably not be in a bed any time soon. Noah watches the Lady as she sleeps. She twitches from time to time, sensing the eyes on her. But she doesn't wake up. And Noah doesn't take his eyes off of her. The moon takes full advantage of the opportunity to caress her face. Noah is envious.

It's near impossible now for him to think of her as a child. She has become a complete woman, ready for the world. Ready for a husband she will please, and who will please her. His mind starts to wander and he doesn't rein it in. He wonders what it would be like to hold her, like that. He wonders what her nakedness would feel like against his own. The thought warms him. But he is also filled with guilt and apprehension, knowing the impossibility of it all.

She turns so that she faces away from him. Her back glistens in the night light. She sleeps like a forest nymph with no care for what stirs on the forest floor. She trusts the woods and knows without a shadow of a doubt that she will wake up in the morning. Her bravery is silent once. But it is easily seen when you look for it. She is not made of moss that's for sure. And she would put up her own sort of fight if she needed to protect herself.

But Noah doesn't want to think of her as a fighter, wild and fierce. He likes this docile, vulnerable Sophia who seems so accessible, so in need of every sort of protection. Her beauty takes Noah to places in his head he had thought were long shut. But having spent so much time with her in the recent past, old feelings are starting to stir. And they are fresh and powerful as ever.

He gets under his blanket and turns the other way. The horses move around a little, a late-night shuffle, and then they settle. Noah too shuffles a little but cannot fall asleep. He holds his eyes closed but nothing happens still. He listens to the activity of the night and tries to use it to sleep. Still, sleep eludes him.

Noah tries to go to happy places in his head. He works hard for his first real memory of her. And it was her hand. He remembers her reaching it out to him and them jumping into the fountain with him. She was so pretty. She was so friendly. And even when the others started to avoid her, even some of her own sisters, still she would play with him. And that wasn't the last time.

They swam often together. They swam every chance they got. As they grew older Sophia kept encouraging him to keep his shirt off. She made him very aware of his birthmark so that he could become increasingly comfortable with himself. He did, and so even their friendship became easier. But he never forgot his station. Sophia on the other hand forgot hers often. She was always very reckless.

One day, in particular, stands out in his mind when they were both just twenty. They lay on the bank of the river after a very active time in the water, so they were both exhausted. Sophia rolled over to Noah and started to trace the outline of his birthmark with her finger. He laughed wildly, threatening to throw up. She traced the outline a little harder and the laughing stopped. She traced the chest part of it completely, ending at his hip.

And then she had him turn over. She did the same to the back part of it, ending at his shoulder. Then she put the side of her face on it and fell asleep. There was no warning, no preparation. Sophia simply fell asleep. She slept for the rest of the afternoon, dead entirely to the world. Noah knew that this would not be good for him when they got back. But he let her sleep nonetheless.

Eventually out of pure anxiety he woke her up. She stood up, laughing as though they had actually done something inappropriate. Noah too felt an unnecessary pang of guilt. Sophia always had a way of transferring such things. They ran back up to the house and Noah to the room he shared with his mother. Sophia went to her own room where her own mother was waiting for her. Mary had no way of being any harsher with Sophia save to tell her the same old rhetoric: "Your father will not be pleased, young Lady."

Noah is eventually asleep.

The horses suddenly become a little restless. The sound of their reigns clanging becomes louder and louder as they lift onto their hind legs. They move around in a panic, trying to free themselves of the trees they are attached to. Noah thinks he is dreaming at first but soon realizes that he isn't.

He gets up quietly and goes to the animals. He rubs them down, trying to relax them. He speaks to them. Nothing works. He looks around, straining to see in the dark, his eyes not yet adjusted. He shakes his head with his eyes closed and then after a moment he opens them again. Still, he sees nothing. Then he hears it. From the undergrowth, he hears a soft growl. He hears another. Then he hears another growl, still. He strains to see what it is but really battles. There is nothing to it. He needs to get a log on the fire quickly so that he can see what the danger is, and where.

The horses are going completely mad now, and Noah tries in vain to get them to calm down. He doesn't want Sophia to wake up and panic. He can drive these opportunistic beasts off himself. The log catches a flame at last and he is pleased. They have surrounded my menacing eyes everywhere. He goes closer and isn't sure if they are wolves or foxes. Both could be a potential problem in big enough numbers.

Noah goes for them, trying as quietly as he can to get them to retreat back into the forest. There is after all nothing with them that is food. But perhaps the lingering smell of the dinner on the dead coals is what has brought them here. Noah goes down low and swings wide. He manages to singe a few but it isn't enough to scare off the others. The horses have made enough noise by now, however, to wake up Sophia.

"Noah, what is it?" She rubs the sleep from her eyes and stands up.

"I don't know, wolves, maybe just foxes." He really still doesn't know.

She goes straight for the horses. Her voice is softer than Noah's and for a minute they are calmer. But as soon as she leaves them they are up on their hind legs making the entire night aware of what is going on. Sophia goes to the dead fire and pulls a log of her own. She joins Noah and he lights hers up. Noah doesn't know what to make of her. He doesn't know what to say.

With her flame ablaze she joins the fight. She keeps her skirt down to protect her legs. And then she charges the beasts trying to make a meal of her. She wields wildly and tries to identify what it is that they are fighting.

"Wolves Noah, they're wolves." She is sure.

"Here? How? This doesn't make sense." Noah knows something about the habits of wild animals.

"Well that's what they are, I am sure of it." She goes in with her flame and her words are confirmed.

The horses try harder and harder to free themselves. It would be a very inconvenient exercise if they did. It would set them back in a way that they really don't need right now. Both of them check on the horses, making sure that they are still secured. They are. But they are incredibly anxious. Noah makes a second knot with additional rope just for his own peace of mind.

Then he is on the wolves again. But for some reason, they seem to have absolutely no fear of the fire. They seem determined to get to Sophia and Noah, even the horses. This is incredibly strange behavior. Especially since there doesn't seem to be a shortage of food in the forest, for carnivores and herbivores alike. Sophia doesn't allow herself a moment to feel any sort of fear. She needs to help Noah get rid of this inconvenience that has stolen her from her sleep.

Both of them grab an additional stick, thick pieces of wood to actually use to injure the predators. Using the torches to locate them, they go all out on the attack now. Choosing one animal each at a time, they go for the heads. Delivering massive blows, the wolves start making for the safety of the forest, one by one.

The fight goes on for quite a while, Noah and Sophia not realizing just how many of these things there were. But they persevere through their own exhaustion and keep driving them off one at a time. It seems unnecessary to kill them. It would just result in unnecessary work for them since it was still night and they would have to deal with the corpses before they drew scavengers. So blows to the head seemed to be enough to drive them away, shocked and with egos bruised.

The horses finally start to settle down. The last of the wolves are driven off and Noah and Sophia look like they've been in the fight they've just been in. Both of them throw their torches into the dead fire and it starts to bring itself to life. A couple of fresh pieces of wood make it a fresh, roaring blaze. This further comforts and settles the horses. Sophia too is happy about the warmth and light.

"Let me see that you're not hurt." Noah is concerned.

"I'm fine Noah, thank you though." Sophia is too exhausted to be fussed over right now.

"Your adrenalin is pumping through you right now so that won't even know you've been hurt. And if you fall asleep without doing something about an injury, you might have the inconvenience of infection to deal with come morning." Noah, as usual, is being overly practical Noah.

"I'm alright Noah." Sophia is annoyed.

"Don't be stubborn Sophia." He persists.

She relents just because as tired as she is to be touched, she is also too tired to argue.

Noah makes a careful and thorough examination of Sophia. To his surprise, she has not even a scratch on her. She really fought with a type of experience she shouldn't have. Where could she have learned this, and when? Noah knows that the answers to these questions he won't get tonight. But one thing, Sophia is becoming more and more of a mystery, an enigma almost, as the trip progresses.

She makes an examination of Noah at his insistence. He too has no scars save for a small burn on the upper part of his forearm. She treats it as best she can with medical supplies in their baggage. Then she makes them both a cup of tea. She is sure to make it sweeter than it normally should be since they've both had a bit of an unexpected shock. They say very little while they sip through the first cup.

Noah cautiously requests a second cup and Sophia obliges. They are more relaxed during this cup and conversation comes a little bit easier. Again they are reminiscing about their childhood. Again they are reminding themselves that Sophia might possibly never see her home again. But she takes it boldly and enjoys the conversation for what it is. There is no point now, nor at any other time, for her to feel sorry for herself. It will not serve her in any way.

"You are very full of surprises Lady Sophia," Noah says, shy.

"And you are very formal Noah" Sophia mocks him since they've been friends since they were three.

"It's expected."

"By who"

"Everyone"

"I don't see everyone here, just me and you"

"Still"

"Still nothing, you could be a lord in the morning and I'd still call you Noah, the boy with the map of the world etched on his body by God himself."

"You give my birthmark a very curious status"

"And you don't give yourself enough freedom to just be a man. This trip will be easier on both of us if you're just Noah and I am just Sophia."

Noah has no reply for the noble lady with a carefree spirit she just shouldn't have. What might it have been like if she could be his if he was able to pursue her? What if he was born into a different station? Why was life always riddled with complications so that you always felt like you were doing the wrong thing? Was one meant to resign oneself fatalistically to the hand dealt? God certainly seemed to play very complicated games with the human heart.

Sophia knows that forgoing the formality of their relationship for this trip would actually make things harder for her. The more she is reminded of her familiarity with Noah the more she remembers some of the dreams she entertained when she was old enough to understand what could happen between men and women. But now that isn't possible, not for her and Noah.

But sometimes things don't go the way we want them to. And more often than not life will send us on a journey that makes no sense in the grand scheme of the lives we had imagined for ourselves. Life has a way of making you think that you are in control of your own destiny and then showing that actually, there is nothing that is in your control. It's a cruel method. Life is a cruel master. But all we can do at the best times is to allow life to steer us where it will.

The journey is a sudden concern for Noah and Sophia. They have no idea still exactly where it is they are going. And they also don't know if they should not have been there by now. If that is the case then the situation could already be far worse than they think it is. And unfortunately, they have as yet found nobody to actually help them in the direction of the Blood Baron. They are going to have to do something about it tomorrow. It's time to apply themselves fully to knowing their destination, and to commit themselves completely to getting there, especially since both of them suddenly recall that the trip was meant to be six days...

CHAPTER 5

"ROWAN, THE LETTER", Mary has had it.

"Letter?" Rowan has been expecting this.

"Yes. You said a letter came asking for Sophia. May I see it?" Mary's speaking is calm and measured.

"Of course, I will find it and let you have it." Rowan is trying not to let the panic that is building inside him show.

"No Rowan, I would like to read it now. If you tell me where it is, I will get it myself." Mary is not going to take no for an answer tonight.

"I will get it for you, Mary." Rowan is sweating under his collar, beads on his brow.

"Tonight, Rowan." She is determined.

"Tonight, Mary." He needs to find a way out of this.

Suddenly there is no further conversation during dinner. Rowan seems heavily burdened and the look on his face, of a wounded lion, has returned. But Mary will not let this distract her. She will no longer be influenced by Rowan and his emotions. She is a mother. And she's put her husband before the well-being of her daughter for long enough. She trusted her husband enough to let him send his daughter away without her knowing where to or why. She should have accompanied Sophia and also met the cousins who were suddenly so interested in getting to know her. But she didn't. And so now she needs to be sure that she hasn't made a grave mistake.

After dinner, Rowan immediately goes to prepare for bed. He draws his own bath, something completely out of character for him, and spends an incredible amount of time in it. He insists that it is just to relax and clear his mind because he needs to decide what the surprise will be for the people this year. He always gives his staff and those who work his lands a surprise, over and above an elaborate feast for his birthday. Mary is having none of it.

She leaves him to hide in his bath and goes down to his study. It's a massive room and the letter could be anywhere. She calls her own lady-in-waiting and they start to comb through the room. They start between the bookshelves and between the pages of the books. And then they go through all the drawers. There is nothing that is any surprise to them, Rowan really being all business and family. Then they look under ornaments and artwork, behind paintings and other wall hangings. They even check under the rugs and any piece of furniture with a base wide enough to hide a letter. Nothing!

There is nowhere else in this room that it could be. And there is no other part of the house that Rowan has as his exclusive space. But Mary will keep up her search. She will figure out where he would have hidden the letter. She will try to get into his mind and figure out where he would think is a good hiding place for this new and seemingly severe secret. She will not give up.

Mary gets to bed and finds Rowan already under the covers. He has completely disappeared under the covers and is trying to fall asleep before she starts to question him again. Mary says nothing. She goes through her usual bedtime routine and gets into bed next to her husband. After giving him a light kiss on the side of his face, she turns over and falls asleep. Rowan is thrown by this and finds it very hard to fall asleep now, tossing and turning for most of the night. Mary sleeps through the night.

She spends her time watching her husband closely. Mary is careful to be inconspicuous, knowing that her husband is an extremely capable hunter. He will easily find that he is being watched. But Mary is very careful, and she too has her own set of stealth skills. And so soon enough she has a list of places that she will have a look at once her husband is out of the house.

Mary arranges a hunt for him as a surprise, and also to get him out of the way so that the parts of his birthday celebrations that need to be kept secret from him can be dealt with. Then the search starts. She tries to be thorough, knowing that a frantic search will see her miss something. She carries this search out herself, wanting to concentrate fully. The search takes her the entire afternoon and produces nothing. By the time her husband returns Mary has to abandon her efforts and help him clean up after the hunt, serving them up a hot meal and some ale.

Rowan looks like the hunt was in fact everything that he needed. He is completely exhausted, a little bit scared, but very relaxed. His roaring laugh has even returned. He goes off to get cleaned with the rest of his pack while Mary finishes up with the table. Mary feels a tinge of optimism. When her husband has had a good hunt he tends to overindulge in the ale. And this means that he is a little more relaxed with his tongue. So tonight might just be the night.

Mary leaves them and goes to help the rest of the staff as they continue with the birthday preparations. Sophia always had such an active role to play in this. It was one of her favorite things. But not only is she now not here to help, but she will not be here at all. This is all too much for Mary. And even if he refuses to say it, it is all too much for Rowan as well. So Mary is going to make the best of this opportunity that has now presented itself. She is going to let her husband enjoy himself with his friends for as long as possible.

She prepares sleeping quarters for them for later and informs them as much so that they can relax into the afternoon and evening. Then she instructs the servers to keep them topped with the best ale in the house. More meat is prepared for them and they are left to reminisce on the days of their youth, some of the stories an obvious exaggeration. But they're at that point now where nobody really cares, as long as the tails are exciting and keep the atmosphere high.

It's easy now for Mary to concentrate on the birthday party knowing that later, her husband will be putty in her hands. She is sure that once she has him in bed, in the moments before he falls asleep, she will get him to whisper everything she needs to hear...

For the rest of the afternoon, Mary and most of the staff are distracted by the fact that Sophia won't be here. It is not only a distraction but causes them all a lot of pain and sadness. This year has turned out to be nothing like anybody expected. Rowan Manor has never been so overcome by sadness. Everyone is almost completely overwhelmed.

In her honor, they try to imagine all the crazy suggestions Sophia might have made. And because they understand her personality and her relationship with her father, they come up with really good suggestions that are most like what Sophia might have put forward. But still, her absence is painfully conspicuous.

Still on they go with all that they think that Sophia would have busied herself with. And these new additions to the preparations make the process all the more time-consuming. But anything that continues to keep the memory of Sophia alive in the home is most welcome. So without questioning anything any further, they just throw themselves completely into it.

Mary keeps checking on her husband. To her delight, he has not let up on the ale. She tolerates the raucous sounds of all the men behaving very badly because they are essentially proving to be her allies in setting up her husband. She will be most appreciative of them come tomorrow, if tonight is as successful as she anticipates that it will be. She is very optimistic about the evening and can only allow her optimism to keep her enthusiastic about later.

Nighttime brings the planning to an end. Servants wait on the men showing no signs of letting up on the ale and banter. Mary doesn't mind. She has dinner by herself and then goes up to prepare for bed. She gets into bed and waits patiently for Rowan but he just doesn't come. Hours pass and he still doesn't come. Mary falls in and out of sleep.

When Mary wakes up the next morning her husband is fast asleep, snoring loudly next to her.

Again Rowan has managed to avoid his wife. And again Mary is incredibly frustrated because she has no more infor-mation about her daughter's whereabouts than she did when her daughter left. She decides that she will not be dissuaded, and makes the decision to bring Rowan's birthday forward. She is the one who absolutely needs the distraction. And bringing this massive event forward will really be a distraction.

Invitations go out and messengers are sent to her daughters. In just over a week her house will be filled with the sounds of her grandchildren and Mary is incredibly excited by this. This doesn't remove thoughts of Sophia, but it does distract Mary from trying to figure out what Rowan is hiding. She needs this to just keep her in as high a spirit as she can be. The ultimate benefit of the entire exercise is that she will spend time with her daughters and her grandsons.

The day of the party arrives, and the Manor is filled with a now unfamiliar sound of children laughing. Everyone cannot believe that the spirit is so easily lifted in the Manor, so quickly. The house looks more festive than it ever has for Rowan's birthday. Mary knows that this has a lot to do with everybody's suggestions that they thought Sophia would have made. There is an incredible sense of joy that everybody feels and cannot hide.

The smell of food fills every corner of the house. Cakes and sweets are all over the place, nobody is denied access to them, especially not the children. It is the usual free for all. The musicians also fill the entire house with the jovial sound of festive music. There are musicians in the gardens and even in the kitchens. There is no part of the house that doesn't feel like every festival and Christmas.

All the work doesn't seem to exhaust anyone. They simply throw themselves completely into it and keep piling up the meals. The most important items seem to be cakes and sweets. There are also many rare delights from as far as Paris and London, but even these are not limited to any nobility. Everybody at the feast has access to everything.

Rowan's grandsons are so pleased to have grandfather back and being his old self again. And his sons-in-law are equally pleased. They go on the birthday hunt before all of them become too drunk. And what a magnificent hunt it is. The youngsters are very sad that they cannot go along. But the boys aged ten and over join the party. So off they go, leaving the others to be comforted by their mothers. The very mothers who find this hunt to be a very long one are still worried about their babies on horses trying to kill a fox.

Mary tries to be jovial, she tries to have fun. But her baby's absence is so conspicuous now you can cut it clear through with a knife. She just cannot get over the fact that Sophia is not here. And that she doesn't know where her daughter is even more painful.

Still, she manages a measure of joviality that doesn't raise too many questions. She is everywhere, making sure that everyone is taken care of. There is just no other way to be for the time being.

Upon their return from the hunt, Rowan gets drunk. Very drunk! This is unlike him since he very seldom gets drunk around his grandsons. But drunk he is. And everyone seems to be having a good time around him, even his grandsons.

He plays with the boys and they love it. He gives them more than the usual attention, but this seems about right for a man as drunk as he is. He doesn't even notice that he's doing it, just having a good time with his boys.

But then Rowan gets very amorous and retires to his bedroom. In bed his wife joins him, hoping that tonight will be the night. She tries to be as soft as she always is, but something in her keeps her from her husband. She cannot surrender herself to him. Mary just cannot give herself to her husband.

Rowan doesn't even notice this. He takes her, completely. His love-making is aggressive and hard. It is not anything like she's used to. She tries and tries to acclimatize herself but to no avail. He's determined to get off, several times; but it just takes forever for him to get off the first time.

He doesn't cum for what seems like hours. But Mary is a patient woman and she knows this probably has something to do with all the ale he's consumed. So she lets him continue on top of her with the virility of a stallion. She will wait him out.

But then she suddenly can't take it anymore. She asks for a reprieve and is given one. Mary offers Rowan a drink, which she spikes. But even when she spikes his drink he continues. He continues until eventually, he passes out from sheer exhaustion. But it doesn't last long and soon enough he is awake again. But he is too tired to make love, much to his wife's relief. She tries for conversation.

"That was interesting", she says.

"Good interesting I hope", is the reply.

Then silence. She has no idea how to ask what she wants to ask but she knows that she will ask it soon. She has to. This not knowing is driving her crazy and she cannot take it anymore. One more day of this and she will surely go mad. She will surely go mad.

But how do you approach a subject that its owner has abandoned?

"Sophia would've enjoyed tonight", she says eventually; finally plucking up the courage to say something. She braces herself for a brazen response that doesn't come.

"Don't start with that again, please, not tonight", is the candid response she receives instead.

She takes it, but Mary knows she must keep trying. She knows she must or else she will lose her mind. It doesn't matter what her husband thinks. It doesn't matter how angry he gets. She is going to get to the bottom of this tonight!

She gets out of bed. There are a million and one things going through her head but she is focused on just the one. She throws her robe over her shoulders and walks to the window. Mary soaks in that time of night when you're not sure if it's about to be morning or if it's late at night. Then she turns to her husband.

"Where is she Rowan, Sophia?" Mary asks.

"Mary!"

"Where, Rowan?" Mary is determined. There is no other way. She will get her answer, no matter what. She will get her answer.

"Nowhere, Mary, she's with her cousins. She is with her cousins," is Rowan's response.

"Where?" Mary asks, determined that she will get an answer regardless.

Rowan stands up. He gets out of bed and joins his wife near the window. He tries to hold her, silence her. He tries in vain to silence her, tries in vain to quiet her down. There is no silencing Mary.

She asks Rowan again where her daughter is. Rowan denies the fact that Sophia is anywhere but with her cousins. He tells her what he wants her to hear. She asks him again. Again he tells her that Sophia is with her cousins.

Mary is having none of it. She wants to know where her daughter is, and she wants to know now. She isn't even sure what she thinks he might say that will placate her, not sure what she needs to hear. But she knows that it is not that Sophia is with her cousins.

"Where is Sophia, Rowan?" she asks with determination.

This is her baby. Sophia is her youngest child. And although she is a woman now, Mary cannot help the way she feels. It's as if the fate of the whole world hangs on the answer she will get to this simple question. Her world threatens to implode, but she must get an answer.

Mary doesn't want to fight. She just wants to know where her daughter is so that if she needs to fetch her, she will. After all, if this is the effect it has on Rowan, what must it not be doing to her daughter? This is her biggest and most sincere concern!

But then he is silent. Rowan goes the kind of silent that makes you want to say something and yet not. It's the kind of silent that makes Mary say something.

"Where is my daughter, Rowan", Mary asks.

He lets her go and creates some distance between them. There is no way for him to be close to her anymore. There is no way for him to create the very closeness that they had just enjoyed; the closeness that he hoped would distract her from Sophia. But nothing distracts Mary from Sophia.

"Where is my daughter, where is Sophia", she asks again.

Again he is silent. Again he keeps what he knows to himself. Again he hides the truth from the one woman who has never kept a secret from him. He just doesn't know what to say.

But Mary is persistent. She won't back down. She knows that if she is going to get any closure on this matter it would have to be tonight. There is no way that she is going to back down; not now.

Then Rowan approaches her. He places his hands on her shoulders. He gives them a squeeze before wrapping his arms around her from the back. She tries to get out of his grip, but not too hard. Then he begins to tell her everything.

Mary isn't shocked, not at first. She knew in that place that knows that her daughter hadn't been sent to some cousins. But this was much worse than she could have imagined. She hadn't thought that her husband would do this vile thing.

But he had. And when the magnitude of what he has done settles on her, she lets out a scream that would have anyone think her heart had just been ripped out of her chest. It had...

She has nothing to say to her husband. All he can do is try and quiet her, his hand gently over her mouth. But Mary pulls his hand away and screams, not at him, not at anyone. She just lets out a scream for everything that her daughter must be going through.

Mary pulls away from Rowan. He lets her go. She starts pacing the room, speaking to herself in French. She wants her child back, now. No matter the damage is done to her already, she knows she can fix it. She will fix it!

She leaves the room, unsure of where she is going. Rowan follows her, but at a distance. He doesn't want to touch her now. He knows that this will aggravate her further. At least she seems to be moving away from where the party still seems to be going on. Mary pushes through the side door that leads to a private garden and sits on one of the benches in the center of it. She starts to say a prayer.

Rowan can only look at his wife. He knows he has done a terrible thing. But did he have a choice? He doesn't think so. Yet now, looking at Mary, he has to consider that perhaps there was another way!

They stay in the garden until the first light of dawn, saying nothing to each other. Then Mary gets up and walks past Rowan, who gives way. He watches her disappear down the hallway, leaving him to think about his sin.

Mary goes back to their bedroom and gets into bed. She tries to control it, but can't help how much she is shaking. She pulls the covers over herself. Still, she shakes. She throws the covers off her, hoping that this will make a difference. It doesn't. Instead, the breeze coming in through the windows makes her shake even more.

She has a lot to consider. But how can she do anything without going against her husband? And as much leeway as she is given with Rowan, he is still her master. How can she go against him? But Sophia is her child. And how could she possibly leave her in the house of the Blood Baron, alone and abandoned?

There was just no way...

Meanwhile, Rowan walks the private garden alone, not sure if he has not lost his wife also. All he knows is that he cannot approach her just yet. But the longer he waits, the longer she has to think about whatever she is thinking about. And that is probably how to get her daughter back from the Blood Baron.

But Sophia has bigger problems at the moment. She has been taken from her room against her will. And now she finds herself in a whorehouse. This could only mean one thing. But that is something she is not ready for, something she's not designed for. It's something she wouldn't survive.

She is at her wit's end, but she maintains her composure. She can think of no other way to be. If they want her they can have her. But she will not be giving them the satisfaction of a performance. She knew when they walked the streets that the looks she was getting were not good. Sophia knew that they were going to try something, she just wasn't sure what. Well, now she knew!

Sophia knows that the Blood Baron won't accept her if she is no longer a virgin. And this bothers her because if she isn't sure when she arrives there, there's no telling what will happen to her family. She's already made a sacrifice for them, taking herself willingly to the Baron. Now if he rejects her...

Rowan finally gathers the courage to approach his wife. The party has died down and nearly everybody is in their sleeping quarters. He has to be very careful of upsetting Mary because otherwise she will rouse the whole house again, and the last thing he needs is for his friends to know what he has done. He'll deal with his own daughters when they find out. But his friends!

He enters the room and shuts the door. Looking at his wife on the bed, curled up like a child, he can't help but want to hold her. But he knows that he is the reason for this so he goes to the dresser and sits down. He picks up Mary's brush and cleans it because she is religious about cleaning her brush after her nightly brushes. Rowan strokes the brush, wishing that it was his wife's face, wishing that she would make him make her feel better; but how?

Rowan sits quietly, knowing that Mary is awake. She is just not speaking to him. And it is killing him. The mighty Rowan who just the day before was on a hunt, having the time of his life, has been brought to his knees. He has to be very humble now with this woman he has hurt so badly.

"Mary, I'm sorry. I just didn't know what else to do..." He manages this feeble statement.

Still, Mary is silent. Even her sobbing has subsided. She is thinking, the way French women do, silently. There just has to be a way to get Sophia back. But how?!

"Mary please say something", Rowan presses.

After what seems like an eternity, she breaks the silence. "What Rowan, what do you want me to say". She isn't screaming or shouting.

"I don't know; anything".

"Well, you gave my baby away without my consent, without my knowledge, Rowan. That is all I can think about right now."

"And would you have agreed had I told you? Would she?" Rowan too isn't shouting, realizing that he has no right to!

"What do you think?!"

Mary turns to face her husband for the first time since he's entered the room. He looks every bit like the broken man that he is. His wounded lion façade has returned. But now Mary knows why.

"We can't leave her there Rowan, you know this. We just cannot abandon our little girl." Mary says it like a statement not a question and this scares Rowan.

"What can I do against the Blood Baron, huh?! I had no choice, Mary!"

"You always have a choice, Rowan. You always have a choice!"

CHAPTER 6

NOAH AND SOPHIA are relieved when they come across another village. But the closer they get to it they realize that it is nothing like the previous one. As they enter they are met with menacing looks that immediately make them wish that they had gone a different route. Noah is watched with deep concern, the men wanting to see exactly who he is and what he is capable of. Sophia is looked at with pure hunger.

Every instinct tells them to just get out of there. But they do need to rest. They do need to get at least one night's rest so that they can move with more speed. This is no time to be afraid of anything. They are going to need to steel themselves against the stares and be sure that every one of their steps has a definite purpose. Both Noah and Sophia decide to look like they are not to be messed with.

They find a room in an inn just to get off the street. Still, they don't feel very safe. Noah is worried about the horses that are left outside. This is going to be a very long afternoon and an even longer night. But they need a comfortable bed, and they decide that they will sleep in stages, checking on the horses and getting some rest. Noah gives Sophia longer sleep sessions, which she hates him for when she wakes up.

The horses are restless often and Noah checks. When it is Sophia's watch, she wakes Noah, upon his insistence. It makes no sense for her to go outside to check. They both know that they are not safe at all here. It feels that morning takes forever to come. And neither of them is rested by the time the sun has risen. All that is on their minds is getting as far away from here as possible, as quickly as possible.

To their surprise, the innkeeper's wife brings them breakfast.

"Slept well?" she asks.

"Yes", Noah lies.

"No! Not at all!" Sophia is more honest.

"Why, what was the problem dear?" asks the innkeeper's wife.

"I don't know. I just get a strange feeling around this place." Sophia is again being honest.

"Nothing to worry about dear. We just don't get many people moving through these parts so you're a bit of a treat."

"Treat?" Noah asks.

"Eat your breakfast now", is the innkeeper's wife's way of dodging the question.

Once they have cleaned themselves up and readied for the journey they enter into the village. They take a moment to see if there are any weapons for sale. They find none. But what they do hear is a lot of talk about the Blood Baron. He's clearly been here more than once and it has never ended well for the village. Even the way they speak of him is in hushed tones, almost as though he can somehow hear them.

As much as they want to get out of here, they could get some information about where the Blood Baron lives. So it would serve them to perhaps stay just one more night. They make their way back to the inn and secure their room for one more night. Then they decide to actually just rest up during the day. They will risk the pubs later when people usually have a lot more to say. The innkeeper offers that they keep their horses with his until they leave.

Noah is half asleep, half awake. Sophia is completely and utterly asleep. He dreams of a father he never knew. He recalls some of the tales his mother told him about his father. Some of them were good, some not so good. But he needs to remember, the good with the bad if he is to have an all-around memory of his father. He wants to remember his father...

He remembers how once, his mother told him that his father was a warrior. That he was in charge of a large army, and that he was fearless. He remembers the tale well, recalling even the parts of it he no longer believed.

His father is said to have been fearless. But as fearless as he is said to have been, he is said to have been ruthless. And tales of his ruthlessness outweighed tales of his fearlessness. Not that Noah's mother would ever let him know this, even when he had grown up and become a man. There was just no way she was going to let her son know just how evil his father was, and that they had in fact run from him all those years ago.

Noah and Sophia ready themselves for the night. Noah advises Sophia to cover up as much as possible since she insists on going with. Actually, he is pleased that she has made such an insistence because he will then be able to keep an eye on her. The town is menacing a disturbingly sinister air about it.

As they walk through the town, Sophia finds that she is on the receiving end of stares; the kind of stares that would make you more than a little uncomfortable. Sophia is uncomfortable. Still, the men look and gawk at her as though she was meat hanging from a butcher's hook. She eventually can't take it anymore and asks Noah if they can leave.

"Leave? But we haven't gotten the information we need yet!" Noah replies.

"Leave it, Noah. Let's just get out of here!" Sophia is really uncomfortable.

"But it's night Sophia, and..."

"Noah let's just go, now!"

Noah sees that there is no point in arguing with Sophia and he heads back to their room. He leaves Sophia in the room, packing up, while he goes and gets the horses. But they're not there. The horses are just not there. Noah goes to find the innkeeper...

He finds him drunk; too drunk to question. But he has to and so he does. The innkeeper just keeps saying that he has no idea. He has no idea why their horses are missing. He has no idea why his horses are still there. He has no idea where Noah can start looking. He just has no idea!

"Why don't you stay and have a drink with me, and we can figure this mess out!" he says.

"No thanks", is Noah's response and he leaves.

But Noah will not give up. He can't! He must find the horses and get them out of there. It's what Sophia wants. It's what she must get. He still isn't quite sure why she wanted to leave, but now he knows that it's best if they do. If only he can find their horses...

He searches the enclosure again, not finding them. He goes from store to open a store in their street, but nothing. Noah gets to some residences but they too don't know about the horses. It's as if they just vanished into thin air.

And it really is. The village is small enough for Noah to traverse from end to end in less than two hours. He gets no joy from anybody regarding his horses and, in fact, feels that finding them might be more of a problem for him. He gets a distinct impression that he does not want to find his horses.

He starts to make his way back. The mood is even more sinister than before. Men are making their way out of their houses and out of pubs, looking at him as if he has just stolen something. He avoids their eyes, nervous. Even though he is the one who has been stolen from, he avoids looking at anybody directly in the eye.

Some men even make contact with him, inviting him to the pub. Noah doesn't know whether to say yes or no, not knowing which will offend more. He remembers Sophia, thinking of her in the room by herself. He wonders if she's okay, or if she will be should he decide to go in for a drink. But soon enough it becomes clear that he has no choice. He has to go in for a drink with the lads. They just won't take no for an answer. He can only hope that Sophia is safe!

Inside the pub, Noah receives stares much unlike the stares Sophia got. But it is enough to make him very uneasy. He sips his ale begrudgingly, not wanting to be drinking just then. He needs to get Sophia out of here. And without horses, that is going to be a task that requires all his senses. So he sips slowly.

The time passes by quickly and soon Noah is being offered another pitcher of ale. Refuse as he does, they let him know that that isn't an option. He takes it, knowing that he needs to get back to Sophia before she came looking for him. Sophia on the streets late at night all alone was not a good idea, not here.

He eventually makes his escape; but not until they've managed to get five pitchers of ale down his throat. Now he hurries to Sophia, hoping that she isn't too mad at him. He hopes that she is safe and that even if she is mad, she is there. He hopes she hasn't gone off looking for him in the middle of the night; or worse, that she doesn't think he left her in that god-forsaken place. Noah just hopes that Sophia had the sense to wait for him in the room.

They can make a plan for horses in the next village. That's what Noah reasons. He reckons that they can make it to the next village on foot. And that provided that the next village is nothing like this one, they will be able to get some rest...and horses!

He eventually reaches the inn. Downstairs is the innkeeper, looking a little more sober. It's amazing what a few hours of sleep will do. He actually looks very sober indeed. So again Noah asks him about the horses. But again he denies knowing anything about them.

Instead of letting him go, however, he offers him a pitcher of ale. He insists that Sophia is okay and that she is sleeping in the room. He insists that he and his wife checked on her just an hour ago and that she was very sleepy. He insists that they left her fast asleep in the room and that he will just disturb her. Noah finally gives in and the innkeeper pours them both a pitcher. He leads him off to a little room that serves as his parlor, and they settle in for their drinks. But Noah is still worried about Sophia and needs to see her.

He indulges the innkeeper just a little while longer and then leaves. Noah makes his way up the stairs, much to the innkeeper's frustration. The innkeeper tries, in vain, to hold him back.

But halfway up the stairs, he bumps into the innkeeper's wife, who insists that Sophia is fine and resting. Now Noah knows there is a problem. He knows that there couldn't possibly be a way that both the innkeeper and his wife would be so concerned for Sophia that they would have checked on her. He needs to get to her quickly.

He pushes past the innkeeper's wife. She gives way easily. Noah rushes up the stairs and turns into the passageway. He looks at their door at the end of the long hallway and prays. He prays to himself that Sophia is safe and asleep inside.

Noah goes down the long hallway, alone. The innkeeper and his wife have disappeared. He gets to the door, his heart racing, every part of him sweating. He takes his hand to the doorknob; turns it. He enters the room.

Sophia is not there!

He doesn't need to search the room. He just knows that she isn't hiding in the cupboard or under the bed. Noah knows in his heart that Sophia has left this room, and it has not been of her own accord. She didn't want to go. There is no way that she would have wanted to go.

But maybe she is just out looking for him. He knows this can't be the case otherwise why would the innkeeper and his wife have lied about seeing her safe and sound in her room. This just got very serious very quickly, and Noah knows he needs to find Sophia, and fast!

First the horses, now Sophia, this was quickly becoming a crisis. Noah needs to get his wits back quickly. He doesn't care too much for the horses anymore, just Sophia. And then they will get out of here. Noah can't help but hope that Sophia is simply out looking for him. But he knows this isn't true.

And it isn't!

She had started to pack as Noah had said, while he went to get the horses. Then the innkeeper's wife came upstairs to her and started chatting. She continued packing for a while before asking the woman to leave so that she could finish up. Then suddenly the innkeeper's wife became slightly agitated with her.

The more she insisted she leave the more agitated she became. Until she stood up and started unpacking Noah and Sophia's things. At this point Sophia knew that something was wrong; very wrong!

"What are you doing?" Sophia asks.

"Oh don't worry my dear, you won't be needing these where you're going", comes the sinister reply.

The innkeeper's wife continues to unpack the things, Sophia just looking on, shocked! But then her senses return and she takes the water bottles from the woman who has invaded what is essentially her space.

After a short tussle, the innkeeper's wife loses her patience and slaps Sophia to the ground. It is a hard slap. The kind you'd expect from a man. But then again, this woman closely resembles her husband.

Sophia stays down, nursing her lip. She knows better than to take on this woman. She prays that Noah will come through the doors at any moment and save her. But he doesn't.

He is stuck at a pub with some menacing locals who aren't taking no for an answer. They want him drunk. They want him so out of it that he can't remember the next day what happened the day before, at least not at first. They want him so drunk that they can get him out of town and leave him in the forest to the wolves, or bandits. Alternatively, they want Noah so drunk that he cannot fight back when they kill him!

But Noah doesn't get that drunk. Even with the innkeeper's ale he still has his wits about him. And that is saying something. He can take his beer.

The room is bare, like the day they moved into it. All their possessions have disappeared, and with them, the innkeeper and his wife. Noah knows not to go looking for them. He has a priority to find Sophia now. Everything else will be sorted out at the next village, thanks to the money bag he has concealed.

He leaves the room and falls into the street. He is sober now, any trace of the night's escapades left with nothing in the room. Noah knows not to ask outright for Sophia, so he just wanders the streets, looking.

Sophia in the meantime has been removed from the inn. She is in a house surrounded by the men that took her from the room. She is being gawked at and teased, but she remains composed. These men will not get the satisfaction of her putting up a fuss. Whatever will be will just have to be.

She thinks of Noah, and her parents. She remembers her upbringing and how her father had made sure that she was shielded from this world. She can't even remember her parents or anybody at their house discussing this world. Sophia is almost enthralled by it, the viciousness of it all. But then she remembers that she is the one who is out of the cauldron and in the fire!

But the men don't touch her. They just tease her. She wonders if this is all some elaborate initiation into the village. She knows it can't be, not with the way the innkeeper's wife treated her. And their possessions are probably being distributed while she stands here being gawked at. Sophia wonders where Noah is. Why hasn't he come to get her yet? Does he even know where she is? Is he even alive?

Noah is very much alive! He goes into a pub, the first one of just two in the back of beyond. He orders up a pitcher of ale and sits alone, scouting the place. Not everyone in the town can be in on the conspiracy against them. So he just waits.

Soon enough he is joined by four burly men, travelers too. He lets the conversation flow for a while until he is sure that they are not a part of this mess. Then he lets them know what's happened, first with the horses, and now with Sophia. But they are too drunk for this drama and they leave him by himself again.

Noah doesn't have time to think, not anymore. He leaves the pub without finishing his drink.

By now it was well past midnight. Noah is anxious, wondering if Sophia is still in the village. He disappears into the shadows, knowing that he has a better chance of finding her with himself hidden. He goes to the other pub and peeps in. Nothing!

Noah now starts to comb the village, house by house. He peers through windows and around corners. Dawn is fast approaching though, and he won't be able to stay hidden for too long. But he has barely covered half the houses!

Sophia is moved to another house. She tries to take in everything, stairs, doors, windows, etc. She takes in smells and tries to decipher what they are. She has already counted how many steps it took her from the previous house. And she knows which way is out of this village.

She doesn't understand how a place could be so lawless. There is no sheriff, well not that she's seen, and everybody seems to be able to do as they please. Even the children have a menacing look about them.

Inside this house is different. It smells different. There is one door from what she can make out, and stairs. There are rooms everywhere, not unlike an inn. But from the outside, she gathered that it was just a normal village house. She could not have been more wrong!

Sophia is in a whorehouse!

The only one in town, it services the entire village. It also services passersby. She notices the girls now, falling out of the rooms with the tricks, some going in. And here she thought it was just a boarding house. The joy of naivety!

That's why this house smelt different. It reeked of sex. And since Sophia hasn't had sex yet, how could she possibly know what it smelt like!

Back at Rowan Manor, it is Mary now who is the recluse. Her daughters tend to her needs while their sons' fathers take care of them. She refuses to come out of the room. And she won't say what is bothering her. She just remains under the covers and refuses to eat. So her eldest just brushes her hair while throwing their father a questioning look. It's too much for the Frenchwoman.

Mary has decided not to say anything to her daughters. But she will feel everything that this revelation makes her feel, and she will feel it in the confines of her room. If only the girls would leave her alone to think. She needs to think.

"Girls, I'd like a moment with your mother please!" Rowan seems to be his old self.

The girls leave, although the oldest one looks at her father with suspicion. Something he said last night made their mother this way, she is sure of it. But what?

He gets on the bed next to his wife.

"Mary, thank you for not saying anything to the girls." He speaks in whispers, as though they are at this very moment listening in on the conversation. They aren't of course. Rowan's daughters have too much respect for him and their mother to do that.

Again Mary starts off by giving her husband the silent

treatment. But this lasts only as long as it takes for her to clear her throat.

"It isn't for you that I keep silent, Rowan. It's for me, so I can think. Can you imagine what will happen if they find out... so no, it's not for you," she says.

"But still, thank you!" He looks broken, but only with her, only with Mary. This is the only place where he will now allow himself to appear defeated because he has somehow broken Mary too.

But Mary is a strong woman. This will not be the end of it. She is down for the moment, the shock of it all too much. But she will figure out how to get Sophia back from the Blood Baron!

Sophia is taken to a room to rest. She has her lip seen to and then is encouraged by the other girls to sleep. She has a choice of little else at the moment, so she does.

Meanwhile outside dawn has broken through the safety of the night and Noah is practically out in the open. He hides in an abandoned shed, hoping that nobody comes in here for anything. The race to find Sophia is brought to an abrupt end, Noah needing to take cover in case someone sees him. And while Sophia rests remarkably peacefully, he is anxious, nervous that he might never get her out of here. But mostly he is just anxious about not seeing her again...

CHAPTER 7

THE HOUSE SMELLS LIKE SWEAT. And incense. And sex. Not that Sophia would recognize the last smell. But it is there, heavy in the air like the heavy curtains on the windows. Sophia drifts in and out of sleep, not sure if she is dreaming.

She half remembers being taken from the room. She half remembers the men who came in after the innkeeper's wife was finished. She half remembers a lot of things that may or may not have happened.

Looking around her, Sophia sees that the room is sparsely furnished. It's a little bit more than the inn room but barely. There's the bed she's on, and a dresser with a large mirror, which was absent at the inn. A sofa to one side of the room is the only piece of furniture that seems out of place in the bedroom, given the state of the village. It's as though she has been transported magically into a whole new world by this piece of furniture.

Sophia manages to get out of bed. She has no idea how long she's been in it. She gathers that it can't have been that long since it is still dark outside when she looks out of the window. Or maybe it's the next night, she can't be sure. Sophia has drifted in and out of sleep for little more than an hour.

She tries the door, surprised that it gives way easily. She peers out into the corridor, doors to the left and right of it. A man stumbles out of a room, obviously drunk. Sophia goes back into the room and waits for the ensuing commotion to die down, something about him being too drunk to get it up but he still has to pay.

Carefully she peeps out of the door again. Silence! The commotion seems to have moved on. Sophia walks out into the passage. Whispers fill her head so that once again she isn't sure if she is dreaming.

Sophia turns into a parlor, where most of the whispering seems to be coming from. There are at least eight women in various positions, discussing the night. The discussions confirm for Sophia what she feared. She is in a whorehouse!

As she turns to look for an exit, she finds herself in the clutches of a man, tall, beefy, stropping. He would be handsome if she had seen him anywhere but here. He might have been handsome had he not turned her right back around and placed a grubby paw on her mouth. She wants to bite the hand that is practically in her mouth now but realizes the futility of it all when suddenly and out of nowhere she is surrounded by three more men.

The women laugh, too tired for any other emotion. They go right back to their conversation while Sophia is taken back to her room. Suddenly everything smells like man, sweaty and unkempt. Sophia hates it immediately.

"Oh precious, trying to get away?" The voice is that of an older woman.

Sophia doesn't answer because she really doesn't know

what she was trying to do. All she can think of now is Noah, wondering if he is even still alive.

The woman is joined by a few others, much younger than she is except for one. The second older woman is kindly, mild-mannered, almost like a grandmother. But she proves to be nothing like a grandmother; at least not like Sophia's grandmother; or any grandmother that she knows.

The younger women hold Sophia down on the bed. It's remarkably comfortable without all the covering. They lift her skirt. She resists, but only briefly. Then her underwear is removed. She wants to fight but knows that this will be futile. She just surrenders to whatever is about to happen to her.

The second older woman positions herself between Sophia's legs. Her fingers are cold and intrusive. She proceeds to invade her like she's never been invaded before. Not too much though, but enough for her to know that the young woman shaking on the bed, being held down against her will, is a virgin.

The examination seems to take longer than necessary. The sun has started to come out through the crack in the curtains where Sophia peeped earlier. It makes contact with her face, the sunlight. And Sophia knows that it's morning. She knows now that she's been in the house a full night.

Then the younger woman holding her let her go, and immediately she curls up in the fetal position. She hugs herself tightly, too tired to worry any longer about what is thought of her. She is just too tired to think of anything; anything but Noah that is. Again her mind wanders, wondering if he is still alive and if he is looking for her.

That she is a virgin never bothered her before. Not until now. She wonders what this means, although deep down she knows. She knows that at any time now she will be handed over to a man who will take it from her and that there is nothing that she can do about it. She hugs herself even tighter.

"You've been a good girl, haven't you miss?" The second older woman suddenly sounds anything but like a grand-mother. Sophia doesn't answer. There really isn't anything to say. She has started to give up on Noah, or anybody for that matter, finding her. Saving her!

As the room becomes busier she looks up to see what they are doing. Water for a bath has been brought in, along with a change of clothes. She can see a pretty young thing admiring the dress that is obviously meant for her. She notices the first older woman busying herself with a bag. It seems to be the magical kind with no bottom because out of it come a million things, everything from perfume to rouge.

It's clear that Sophia isn't going to get much rest.

She puts herself in the bath and scrubs herself clean, scrubbing away all that is still going to happen to her. Sophia doesn't stay in the bath longer than she needs to. She exits the basin and watches, wet, while it is taken away.

A young woman called Rachel comes up to her to dry her. She pulls back, drying herself instead as much as she can, and as fast as she can. Standing naked in front of these strange, lost women seems normal now. Or maybe Sophia is just past caring. She eventually lets Rachel dry her hair.

The day seems to drift by unconcerned for Sophia. She is served breakfast at what seems like lunchtime, and only because she looks like she can't take it another minute more. She is being primed, color on her face placed there and then removed, only to be replaced by a different color. The first old lady, who by this time has introduced herself as Hazel, seems determined to get Sophia's look just right.

After breakfast, or lunch, or whatever it is, Sophia once

again has her face replaced. Her lips are a deep red, her eyes smoky. She has more blusher on than she'd like and resembles a caricature of herself. With the dress on, the look is complete, save for her hair. They get into that last, not expecting it to be quite so soft. She resembles a courtesan. And for all intents and purposes, that is exactly what she is.

Again she wants to sleep, hoping that this will all fade away into a dream and she will wake up with her mother brushing her hair. She remembers Noah again and thinks that even waking up next to him in the middle of the forest would be better than this. But with her look finally just right, the last thing that will happen now is sleep.

Four men are in the parlor. Sophia is presented to them, looking overdone and whorish, but they seem to approve. "So you're sure she's a virgin," asks a pale white face with a shirt on that's a few sizes too big. "Sure sir," comes the response. Sophia doesn't know where the response comes from, feeling like it's just her and the four men in the room. When the door closes behind her, it is!

The men look her over with hungry eyes, desperate for a taste. Even through the heavy makeup, they can see her skin is soft. And in her eyes, they can tell that she has never been touched by a man, not like that. Sophia is afraid, more so than she would like to admit to herself. But she stares her captors down, daring them to do whatever it is that they want to do with her.

They are hungry for her virginity. But even hungrier for the price it will fetch. After they get her to sit down they huddle on the couch discussing the handover. 'He will be pleased with her' she hears them say, and wonders who 'he' is. Then they drink their ale with her still in the room. She has never drank the stuff but she knows that unless there is an occasion, it is too early to be consuming the ghastly brew.

She watches them drinking for a while, and then Hazel comes in and takes her away. "She needs to rest up before tonight" is all she says to the four while guiding Sophia out of the room.

She is placed back in her room, her dress removed, and the makeup is taken off her face. She sees the bottles and jars on the dresser, so she knows she will have to go through it all again in a little while. Naked but not cold, she gets on to the bed and listens to the door locking outside. In a few hours, she will lose her most prized possession, her virginity. So she rests up, not even sure how this will happen. She falls asleep not thinking of Noah but wondering who 'he' is, and hoping that at the very least, he will be kind. She wonders if she tells 'him' that she was taken against her will if it will make a difference. Finally, exhaustion takes its toll and she is soon fast asleep.

Noah knows that it is dangerous to look for Sophia during the day, but if she is still in the village then he is determined to find her. He manages to wait it out until after lunch when things seem to take on a jovial atmosphere. Everyone is very quickly becoming drunk, at least everyone who is giving him the evil eye, and Noah stirs from his hiding place-a pigsty.

Frantically he begins to search for Sophia, avoiding as best he can the people he met the night before. But this village seems to be getting smaller and smaller, and Noah seems to be moving around in circles. He gets a cape eventually, from a tradesman passing through, but this just seems to draw more attention to him, especially with the sun beating down from above. He tosses it, deciding that he will find her no matter what, and there isn't a thing that anybody can do about it.

He starts knocking on doors, pushing his way inside.

The first few are empty except for the women of the house, and they have not seen her. He checks under bales of hay. Just in case, and where he finds a trap door, he investigates. Word spreads quickly in the small village of the madman who is looking for his lost love.

It gets to her captors, the news that Noah is still in town and that he is leaving no stone unturned in his search for her. They rally a few men who will let him know that they will have none of it. This is their village, their way of life. And Noah had no business passing through this way. He had no business delivering up a tasty morsel like Sophia to them.

The men become angry with him for not giving up. They hunt for Noah, while he continues to look for Sophia. Many close calls, too many, and he is soon back with the pigs, hiding, waiting for nightfall.

The hours suddenly drag on. Noah looks up at the sun which has not moved from its current position in the sky. He waits, wondering. At least he knows that she must still be in the village if they want him gone. He imagines all sorts of things that they might be doing to her right now but quickly dismisses them. He will not think of that. He must just find her and get her gone from this wretched place.

Sophia meanwhile is asleep. She moves through dreams of Noah, dreams of her family, and the life she left behind. Every one of the dreams she has about Noah end with him dead and she starts, awake. But soon enough she is sleeping again and dreaming, having accepted her fate.

Sleep will not come for Noah, how can it? He is now a wanted man, a fugitive in this village that he has never ever been to. The pigs' smell, sniffing him to the point that he thinks they might just eat him. He cowers in the corner, under their shelter, watching the animals throw themselves around in the mud just to cool down.

After what feels like forever, Noah stirs from under the shelter. He isn't sure if the pigs are sleeping but still he carefully creeps between the large animals, trying not to touch them in case they wake up. Pigs are loud, but thankfully the owners didn't care much for them except to feed them, which they had done prior to Noah using the sty as his hideout.

By now Noah looks as bad as he smells, but there is nowhere for him to clean up. There is no time for it either, not if he is going to find Sophia in time. He resumes his search for her, more frantically as the sun finally begins to set. He knows that the longer he lets her remain with her captors, the less likely he is to find her, at least alive.

Finally, he comes upon the whorehouse, observing it from a distance behind some barrels in an alley. He watches the movements of the men coming and going, hoping that one of them will leave with Sophia, who he hopes is in the house. She just has to be, because there are so few houses left. Noah knows what is going on inside the house. He knows this from the satisfied looks of the men that are leaving it. He wonders how many of these men chose Sophia, the untouched soft beauty from another place, another time.

He can't enter the house looking the way he does, at least not through the front door. He thinks for a minute, but it's a minute too long because just as he stands up four hands are on him. He screams and kicks, but nobody does anything. They just walk by, watching the young man who is apparently fighting for his life, and then move on. Noah is dragged further down the alley and into a room at the end of it.

A punch sends him to the ground, and then he is kicked in his gut several times. He knows now that Sophia must be in the whorehouse, and that he has pissed off the people who took her. Another punch comes from the man now kneeling on both his arms so that the only parts of him that can move are his legs, which he kicks about frantically. Still another punch so that he sees stars momentarily. Then he passes out, briefly.

The men take him from the room and lead him to an open field just outside the village. He has come to but doesn't let his captors know this. He just needs to choose the right time to escape, before they kill him, which is what they discuss on the way.

He does, landing a right hook directly in one man's jaw. He punches the second man in his gut. While the two men try to recover from the unexpected assault Noah runs away. He gets as far away from his assailants as possible without losing sight of the village. It's almost nighttime, and when night falls, he will sneak back into the village to save Sophia!

Night falls. Noah makes his way back to the village, protected by the darkness. He moves through the shadows, a ghost, avoiding everybody he sees. It's hard to do, people already filling the streets and pubs, already drunk. He finds his way to the whorehouse, avoiding the alley that he was attacked in just hours before.

There's a lot of activity tonight, tradesmen passing through for a night's rest and a pitcher of ale. He wants to approach them for help, but he can't be sure that they will help him. He looks like a madman and smells like a beggar. He decides to go it alone.

Noah spots a shed in the yard of the whorehouse, or what's left of it. He decides that this will be a good place to hide while he thinks of a plan to rescue Sophia. The problem with the shed, however, is that from inside it, he will not be able to see the front door. And if they plan to take her out of the house, this is the door they will probably use. But being out in the open the way he is is dangerous. He is a wanted man.

Between the back door and the shed is a well. Noah uses it to get some of the mud off of him, throwing his eyes to the door occasionally to make sure that nobody comes through it. He loses his shirt, leaving him with nothing but his trousers on. The shirt is a mess of mud and blood, and after washing up Noah realizes that most of the blood is his, probably from his earlier attack. He can't think of that right now. He lets the shirt sink to the bottom of the well after he has taken a drink. Then he makes his way to the shed.

The building is old, and it feels like it might come down on him at any moment. Still, he waits inside. Fifteen minutes later he hears a noise and stirs. Nothing. His head must be playing tricks with him. In fact, this whole situation feels like a very long nightmare, one from which he will wake any moment and be back in Rowan's house with Sophia, loving her from a distance until one day his courage allows him to do so up close.

But that will not happen now.

After half an hour Noah comes out of the shed, shirtless and wet, and still smelling somewhat of a pig. He goes around the side of the house where he can see the front door more clearly. He now has a clear view of the comings and goings, and they are many. He wonders how many men have had the pleasure of Sophia yet, but quickly dismisses the thought. He must focus on getting her out of the house.

Meanwhile, inside the house, it's business as usual. Men come, pay, play, and then leave after a drink or two. All the rooms are occupied, it is quite a busy night. Some men hang around the parlor while others sit in the lounge waiting for their turn. It's mostly just passers-through, but a few locals as well, the regular clientele of the establishment.

Sophia wakes up to find herself surrounded by the two old women from earlier.

"Time to get you up miss. Time to get ready. He'll be waiting for you by now!" one of them says. She doesn't know who speaks because she doesn't lookup. They help her off the bed and into the dress. Then her face is plastered on again, this time with more enthusiasm, the woman doing the plastering knowing now just which colors to use. "They'll be here any minute to get you. And you had better be good. He won't like it if you're not!" she speaks almost through her teeth like they've been wired together or something.

Noah spots the two thugs from earlier enter the house. He is happy for the shadows on the side of the house which provide him with a safe hiding place. He can only hope that they've come for Sophia, knowing that her virginity will be prized by one of the few rich men in the village, and knowing that such a man would not want to actually come to a whorehouse. He is right because a few moments later they exit the house with her in tow. She looks scared, even under all the makeup, and even though she tries her best not to appear so.

They move quickly through the streets of the village, Noah keeping a safe following distance. He hides in the shadows like a ghost, drawing as little attention to himself as possible. It might have been easier for him to hide without his birthmark, but it is a permanent fixture, one that draws stares from the few people who see him. He cannot worry about that now, worrying instead about how he is going to get Sophia away from the men who've clearly sold her to the highest bidder.

The men turn up a familiar road, to the inn. Right next to it is a house that seems so out of place in the village that Noah wonders why he hadn't noticed it before. It's modest when compared to Rowan Manor, but not by village standards, and certainly not by this village's standards. The men disappear into the front door and Noah quickly makes for the safety of its side, a large window with the curtains open framing the people inside.

Noah sees the men, and Sophia, in the parlor-like room. Then a man comes in, obviously the owner of the house judging by the way he moves through it. He is also expensively dressed. He offers the men a drink, revealing a gaping hole where teeth once were. You can see that he is large, even under his shirt, and he runs a hand gently over Sophia's face while the men get their own drinks.

"Nice, very nice. We're going to have a good time you and me." He says this to her as though it were supposed to make her feel better about losing her virginity to a toothless, old fool. "Don't you speak," he continues. Still, Sophia is silent, her fight gone. She cannot believe that her life has come to this. "Well no matter, silence is golden, isn't that what they say?" He laughs loudly, and the men too, just because.

Noah wonders if there are any servants in the house. There must be, but he has not seen anyone else. He watches while the men finish their ale, and then watches Sophia alone in the room as the owner of the house lets his delivery men out. They will come for her in the morning.

"Sophia," Noah whispers through the open window.

She doesn't hear him, lost in the land of what might have been but stuck in the land of what is. "Sophia," a little louder this time. She looks up, then around. She knows this voice. But it can't be, can it? Sophia seems to be planted in the spot where she stands, not having taken a single step in any direction since she arrived.

"Sophia," Noah tries again, bringing the young woman out of her dreamland. She looks to the window but sees nothing. Slowly she moves to where the sound of her name is coming, and just as she gets to it, just as she reaches the open window, just as she sees a glimpse of Noah, the tooth-less man returns, still laughing at something that must have been said at the door but that Sophia did not hear.

"Call me Ewan lass," a toothless grin. He is obviously drunk, but not too drunk for Noah to risk taking him on. Sophia remains quiet, hiding her excitement at the fact that Noah is just outside the window, within reach. She just needs to hold on a little longer, knowing that at any moment Noah is going to save her. She cannot think yet how they will get out of the village, but that doesn't matter. What matters for now is just getting out of the house.

Ewan runs his hands over her face as though he doesn't want to ruin her makeup, although she wishes he would. It feels heavy on her face and is starting to irritate her delicate skin. Then Ewan puts a hand under her dress and Sophia falls onto the couch. He follows her down and fumbles with underwear that isn't there. They've made it very easy for him, and he loves it. His hand grazes roughly over her femininity and she squirms, wishing that Noah would hurry things along.

Sophia writhes under the man who is determined to get inside her now. He wants his fingers inside her first but makes a mental note to go gently. Ewan is sure that she is a virgin, the way she tries to get out from under him, completely resists his invasion. She can't help it now. She thought she would be able to let herself go, but now that she is here, she is determined to hold on to her virginity!

Noah knows that he must do something soon. He braces himself, and then climbs through the window, Ewan distracted by the possibility of Sophia. He has Sophia's dress up to her waist now as he fumbles with his trousers. Ewan's bilk is on top of Sophia now such that even with her dress so high up, Noah cannot see the parts of her that she does not mean for him to see.

Noah moves quickly. Just as Ewan is about to reveal himself to Sophia he places a hand over his mouth and lifts him off of her. He is as heavy as he is big, but Noah is determined. So determined is he in fact that he pulls Ewan all the way to the ground, careful not to lose his grip on the large man's mouth. Thankfully they miss anything that might fall over and bring servants into the room. Sophia gathers herself quickly.

She stands over the pair wrestling on the ground. Noah has his forearm around Ewan's thick neck, his other hand still on his mouth. Ewan is lashing out at him with both arms, tree stumps that hit Noah repeatedly in his ribcage. Noah holds out, hoping that his chokehold will send the giant to sleep at any moment. But Ewan is feisty, despite his drunken state. He just lashes out even harder so that Noah is the one losing his breath. The sheer bulk of the man should have knocked him out!

Sophia looks around the room. She goes to the parlor doors and closes them. Thankfully they lock. She locks them and continues her search for something that she can knock Ewan out with. But there is nothing that she can carry on her own, and nothing that she can carry is large enough to have any effect on the man who was seconds away from deflowering her. This is going to have to be Noah's fight.

And what a fight it is! Ewan manages to get Noah's hold on his throat released by turning over. Still, Noah manages to keep his hand over Ewan's mouth, while he holds on to the burly man with his free hand. Ewan is on his knees briefly. Then he stands up and spreads his arms so that Noah loses his hold and goes flying to the sofa. They wait for him to scream, to raise the alarm that will bring throngs of servants into the room, but Ewan is obviously confident in his ability to take on this intruder.

He moves towards Noah with a speed that belies his size. Sophia ducks out of the way just in time. He swings wide and misses. He swings again. Again it is too wide and he misses. On his third attempt he connects his fist with Noah's jaw and Noah stumbles back but doesn't fall. Noah swings low, punching him in his gut several times. But his punches have no effect on the big man!

Sophia goes to the window and shuts the curtain in case anyone is curious enough to peep through. She also closes the window as an afterthought despite the heat. When she turns back to the room she sees Ewan going for Noah, Noah not getting a gap any more to reach his broad frame. She rushes towards Ewan but thinks better of it when he turns towards her and just misses her face with a slap.

Ewan's size is starting to count against him. He swings at Noah more sluggishly now, exhausted from the effort. He tries to catch his breath, both hands on his knees, panting. Noah sees a gap and lands his fist in Ewan's face, one, two, three, four before he too catches his breath. He too now has both hands on both knees. They look at each other, Ewan trying to shout for help. But he can't breathe, so he can't speak let alone shout.

Noah gets a second wind. He takes Ewan's face in his hands and pulls him towards himself so that their heads collide. He staggers back, as does Ewan, and both of them shake their heads, trying to get the stars out. Ewan swings blindly now, trying to get at Noah before he recovers.

But Noah is back on his feet quickly. He moves out of the way and lets the ogre swing at him, tiring him out. Then he goes in to deliver the death blow, and with four more carefully placed fists, Ewan lands on the ground with a thud. Noah checks that he has knocked him out before turning to Sophia, who looks on in disbelief.

There is no time for long embraces. They need to get out of here. They carefully open the window, Noah checking up and down the side of the house. When he sees nobody, he climbs out first before helping Sophia out. She is in shock at being saved, but Noah knows that they are not out of the woods yet. They still need to get out of the village.

They move quickly through the back alleys of the streets, trying to avoid eyes. And they do, for the most part. By the time they reach the outskirts of the village they don't look back. The run!

Noah knows that Sophia must be tired from being captured, and he doesn't know what damage has been done, but there is the need to get as far away from the village as possible, as quickly as possible. They really have no choice.

They reach the forest, and then Sophia has to rest. Noah pulls her just a little further into the woods until he is sure that they are not being followed, and then they stop. Sophia pants keel over onto her knees and then breathes deep. She lies on the ground, finding the earth soft and inviting. It's probably just because she needs to sleep now and rest up after her ordeal. Noah just watches her, letting her sleep, which she does quickly.

There is a moment when he feels compelled to kiss her, but he doesn't. He just watches her until sleep overwhelms him and he too is sleeping on the forest floor. They curl into each other and allow the sound of the night to override their desire to just keep running. They can't anyway, too tired, and Sophia is still a little traumatized by her ordeal. But at least they sleep.

CHAPTER 8

THE JOURNEY HAS REALLY STARTED to take its toll on Sophia. She is exhausted. But they keep on pushing forward. She drags behind, grateful for every break. But the breaks don't last long, since if they had not had the accident, or gone on a complete roundabout, or been held up in the previous village, they should have been there by now!

"I'm tired Noah, really" is all Sophia manages before she keels over and is on her knees. "I know Sophia, but we've got a lot of ground to cover." Noah too is tired, but will not risk the tyrant thinking that they're not coming, especially now that Sophia has made up her mind.

They push on for half the day, not passing anybody along the way, and not seeing any villages in sight. There is still the chance that they might be pursued by Sophia's captors. And so Noah is insistent on getting as much distance between them and the vile men from the previous village as possible.

But then Sophia cannot take it anymore. They've reached a valley and she needs to rest up before they take on the steep ravine that forms the upside of the valley.

Noah allows her to sit, exposed by a stream that runs the length of the valley. There are no trees, no shade, no bushes. But Sophia is so tired that she falls asleep almost immediately.

Noah half sleeps, the sun beating down on both of them. It is as though the sun is determined to extract all the moisture left inside them, so Noah sips regularly from the stream in between sleeps. Sophia is dead to the world so Noah just brings handfuls of water to her mouth, wets the sides of it, and wipes her brow occasionally. She truly is beautiful, even in her current state.

He lets her sleep until nighttime. Then he gently wakes her, and after she has had a drink from the stream, mostly to curb the hunger, they press on. The ravine is steep and really takes its toll on them both, despite the rest that they've had. They are hungry, and hunger has a way of creeping up on you no matter how much water you drink.

When they eventually make it out of the valley they are even more exhausted. They take another brief rest, and then they're on their way. There is really no more time to lose. Too much time has already passed and they are both not sure what this means. What they know is that they are moving in the right direction at least and that within the next few days, more or less, provided they get horses in the next village, they will have arrived.

Anxiously they move forward, through the night. Still, there is no sign of civilization. Both of them are quiet now. Nobody has anything to say to each other. Or if they do, they are not saying it. They just keep their pace, hand in hand, moving towards Sophia's new prison.

Sophia reaches that point where she can't feel her feet. She ignores this, knowing the repercussions of not arriving on time. They've lost a lot of ground, and it's impossible to make it up. But they are pushing forward regardless, trying to get to the Blood Baron as soon as they can.

They notice what looks like plantations. If it wasn't that the crop was faded and wilted wheat, they might have had something to eat. But at least they know that they must be close to a village, which means that they are at least close to human civilization, which is a good thing. They think! They hope actually, given that it is less than a day's journey from their last encounter with 'civilization'. And that didn't go too well!

When the houses start to get closer to each other they hold their breath, not sure what this next village has in store for them. But they are famished. And the thought of going another day without something to eat is one that neither of them can bear.

The village is a whole other kind of chaos. When they reach the market they are grateful that Noah had taken the money bag. But the village market is busy; very busy! They move between the stalls, looking for the shortest line, but they are all equally long.

They choose a line that offers the most variety. It's probably the failed crop that has contributed to these long lines, but they have no care for that right now. Both Noah and Sophia just focus on not dying in the queue before they get to the much-needed food.

In the queue, they attract even more attention than before. Noah has his birthmark exposed without a shirt on, and Sophia's face is still that of a courtesan. She makes a note to clean her face as soon as they have their food, Noah is, unfortunately, unable to remove his markings with water. They eventually reach the front of the queue, although it has taken them half the day.

They purchase a lot of fruit. Surprisingly there is a wide

selection to choose from. Bread and cake too. There is no need for meat as they have to check their appetites, having gone more than a day without food. They choose non-alcoholic ale as well, and then they make for a quiet spot, which is hard to find, given the business of the market. But on the outskirts of the village things quiet down and so they choose a shady spot under a tree.

Sophia and Noah eat slowly, getting more and more animated as they eat. They are really quickly getting the spring back in their steps, although there is not a plan to move for a while. They take a break from eating so that Sophia can clean her face at a nearby stream, Noah washing up too. Then they get back to eating.

Soon they are filled up, and there is nothing left. They consider buying more food for the road, but there is nothing left when they go back to the market. Instead, Noah gets a shirt and Sophia gets a more modest dress, a cooler one too. They purchase a bag and two water skins, filling the water skins at the fountain in the middle of the market. There are no horses for sale, so they get the general direction to the Blood Baron's compound and set off on foot. The sun is already starting to set, so it's much cooler.

Once the sun goes down completely they pick up their pace. Moving like wolves through the forest, they are swift. They move over stones and around hills, not wanting to go over them in case they just get tired again. They cannot deal with any more delays. Hopefully, they will come across another village or two, for food and hopefully horses.

Another full day goes by, with no village in sight. They rest at streams and brooks, Sophia being allowed to sleep while Noah watches over her. Noah sleeps only for brief moments at a time, but by now he is used to it. Once it starts to cool down, as the sun sets, they hit the road again, really covering the ground, making up for the time they have lost.

By the second day they are slowing down again, hunger rearing its ugly head once more. They regret having finished all the fruit at the previous village, but how were they to know that there would be nothing left when they went back. Sophia particularly is taking strain, never having gone a day in her life without food before this trip. It's amazing how many things she took for granted before this. She misses her parents even more as they had truly given her the kind of life that had shielded her from the real world.

And this shielding is not such a bad thing she realizes. Everyone who works for her father is happy, and they definitely have enough to eat. The rumble in her belly lets her know that she certainly is not at home, and her mother isn't going to call her down to dinner any time soon. She will never again be called down to dinner by her mother. The sadness of this realization slows her down even more.

Noah understands. He too slows down and lets Sophia catch herself. They stop when she finally has a total breakdown, just a few hours into their walk. The night does little to hide Sophia from the pain of everything that she has lost.

"I know it's the right thing Noah, I just know it."

"Sophia, it doesn't have to be this way, but you've made up your mind and so there is nothing I can do to stop you."

Between sobs, Noah holds her to him. He smells like the earth after it has rained. She breathes in his scent, letting him go only when she is again overcome with grief and in tears.

"It's okay Sophia, it's okay," he tells her, not sure if he is just saying that it is okay to cry, or if he too hasn't given up trying to get her to change her mind about going to the Baron's house. He wonders how bad he can actually be, despite the stories they've heard on their journey. Noah remembers the warning the first bandits gave them and for a moment he wants to take Sophia away, and look after her somewhere far away. But he knows that she will never be happy knowing that she put her family at risk like that.

There is no time for them to stop the next day, having lost the night to Sophia's weeping. It's hot, but at least there is a soft rain that cools them down while the sun heats them up. There's still no sign of another village.

A caravan approaches on the horizon. There is the fear that they might be kidnapped and returned to the villagers that held Sophia captive, but they're both so hungry that they decide to wait for it by the side of the road. It seems to take forever to get to them, Noah and Sophia are too tired and hungry to go any further to meet them.

"Stop, stop, stop," a young woman sitting up front pulls on her father's arm. He pulls on the reigns and the horses stop reluctantly in the rain. The woman clambers down the wagon and goes straight to Sophia, who isn't passed out but is clearly in need of help.

"Is she okay? Father, water, quickly!" She makes a quick assessment of Sophia and decides that water is what she needs, despite the two recently filled water skins on them.

"Food, do you have any food for us?" Noah asks feebly. He is not too hungry to be embarrassed by their situation. "We can pay you," he manages.

"Don't worry about that. Food, father!" the young woman says, obviously having a serious hold over her father, who brings down some fruit that he had in the front. Then he calls to his wife, who is in the wagon behind theirs, telling her that food is needed.

Sophia grabs the apple she's offered and bites into it three times before she starts chewing. Noah slows her down and she obeys him, embarrassed. He takes a bite from the apple in his hand before thanking his hosts. They both eat their apples really slowly now while the older woman and her daughter prepare their meal. It's lunchtime anyway, so they decide to stop. Thankfully even the rain has stopped, allowing them to start a fire and have a hot meal.

Noah in particular finds it hard to resist eating fast, but he does. He can ill afford the cramps that will follow if he does. He looks across to Sophia, who is sitting with the women, eating slowly, focusing hard, and he smiles to himself. This was a lucky break, one that they may not get again. But how can he ask them for food to help them along with their journey?

"So how long to the next village?" He tries to get an idea of where they are. The vague directions they were given to the Blood Baron's compound put them at two weeks' walk away. They would need at least three or four villages in between, provided they couldn't get any horses. If they can get horses then the trip is reduced to four days.

"Half a day's ride, a bit more on those," he responds to Noah, pointing to his feet with his head.

"Okay…" Noah lets his response settle and this allows his host to give him the response that he wants. He calls his wife to him and she goes off to pack some food up for Noah and Sophia to take with them. They wave at the caravan as it disappears around a bend and then they continue their journey, the rain starting to come down again.

It rains for all the rest of the afternoon, so Noah and Sophia can keep walking. They press on silently, their bellies full, and their heads filled with thoughts of things to come. Sophia is especially distracted by her thoughts.

The sun hangs low in the sky now. It turns red and then pink, and then a deep orange so that they know that it is about to set. Another day lost, but at least they have food to get them to the next village, where hopefully they will find horses.

Day turns to night and they decide to rest a bit.

But it's strange for Noah. He has a strange feeling that they're being followed. He looks around, not mentioning this to Sophia. After all, he sees nothing, hears nothing. So how can he tell her that there's a phantom presence stalking them?

They move on to the next village. It's better stocked than the one before. So they manage to replenish their food stocks. There is even a nicer inn, but taking a whole night out to rest is out of the question. Noah manages to purchase a dagger, presumably to help with the cutting of bread and meat, but he knows what it's actually for.

Again the sunset finds them moving on. They stop for brief moments to eat, to rest, and then they're on the move again. The phantoms seem to be getting closer now, but still he says nothing to Sophia.

Then he hears a growl, low and menacing. And then another one. He stops Sophia, who is moving faster than he is for the first time and is totally unaware of her surrounds. She has one thing on her mind now, and that is to get to the Blood Baron before he thinks she isn't coming. The world around her seems to have disappeared; even the rocks that she has to get over on the road are a mere distraction.

She stops, shaken from her dream world.

"What is it Noah?" She asks, oblivious to all around her except for the road ahead.

"Nothing, I just think we should rest up for a while." Noah's answer is not as convincing as he would have liked it to be. Sophia just shrugs her shoulders and pulls him along, fiercely determined to enter the great unknown. She is tired of wandering out here in the wilderness and tired of wondering what kind of life awaits her at the Blood Baron's. She just wants to know once and for all so she can settle into it. She has given in to what destiny has in store for her. In fact, she gave in a long time ago.

"No, not yet. Come on Noah, just a little more, just a little further."

Reluctantly Noah lets himself be pulled along for a while before he catches up to Sophia and they are walking side by side. Still he can't help the impression that they are being watched, stalked even, on this dark night. The forest is thick and blocks out even the light of the moon, so they tread carefully, their eyes not fully adjusting to the darkness, and they hope they will hit a clearing soon.

They do, and moonlight streams down over them like the rays of the sun. They stop to catch their breaths, Noah listening intently to the sounds of the night. There it is again, a soft low growl. He turns quickly to check behind him but sees nothing.

"What's that?" Noah eventually asks Sophia.

"What?" She really hasn't heard anything.

Noah listens. He too hears nothing now. He stops trying to hear ghosts and takes Sophia's hand. They press on, the darkness overwhelms them. But it's a little brighter than it was in the forest. Still, they press on, Noah practically pulling Sophia along now. She wonders what he heard that has him so rattled.

Then he stops! He looks up, knowing now that he isn't imagining things. He pulls Sophia behind him, protecting her from danger that he himself hasn't seen yet. He wishes now that he had started a fire in the woods, but he knows that it's too late. Noah circles Sophia, his back to her, and waits.

Out of the darkness come eyes; one pair, then two. Before long they are surrounded by eyes, at least twelve pairs, and low growls. Sophia latches onto Noah and holds on tight. He allows this briefly, and then gently shakes her loose, reaching for the dagger, slowly. They're in trouble. And without fire to protect them, he fears the worst. With twelve wolves around them, it won't be long before they become a meal!

There is nowhere to run. If only they could retract back into the safety of the woods, where fallen sticks would provide them with weapons; but in the clearing, there seems to be nothing around them to fend off the attack.

Noah tries to make himself bigger than he is. He raises his arms high above his head, hoping his size alone will intimidate the animals enough to just leave them alone. But these wolves are hungry, and there is no way that they are going to let such an easy meal slip through their teeth.

One wolf can't stand the stalemate any longer. It dives for Noah. Noah manages to punch it in the face so that it falls to the ground with a wince. But it is quickly up again, and again it goes for him. This time Noah lodges the dagger in its head. As it falls to the ground it pulls Noah and the dagger with it. Noah shakes the dagger free from its skull quickly and returns to standing. The wolf doesn't get up again.

The growling gets even louder now. The wolves move closer, angered by the death of their leader. Noah had hoped that this would scare them off but no. And now they are at the brink of an all-out battle with eleven livid wolves.

Noah keeps Sophia next to him with his one arm, the other stretched up high. He brings it low, swaying the dagger in front of the animals, trying to look as menacing as he can. They seem to know that this means danger for them and so none of them dares to charge first. But their growling is louder than ever now, and it seems like they're preparing to come charging all at once!

They need to get to the outside of this circle if they are going to have a chance. They need to get back into the forest where they can either find a weapon or climb a tree. Either option seems viable at the moment. Noah pulls Sophia close to him and whispers in her ear while keeping an eye on their attackers.

"We need to get back into the woods okay. So when I say run, you run."

Noah turns them so that they face the wolves that are blocking their path back into the forest. Sophia tucks her skirt in at the waist, exposing delicate ankles that have seen better days. Everything seems to be happening very slowly until Noah shouts 'run'. And they do.

Noah lunges forth with his dagger and it settles between the eyes of the wolf in front of him. Instinctively the wolves to the left and right of it give way. Noah struggles to dislodge the knife this time, but Sophia is already running. Two wolves are on her tail, catching up with her fast. Noah pulls the knife out just as a wolf dives for his neck. He stands up, the animal hitting against his back instead, unable to get a grip with its teeth.

He doesn't turn around. Running as fast as he can, he catches up with the wolves on Sophia's heels. They've practically got her when he reaches them. He dives for one, inserting his dagger in its back. The other one stops his pursuit of Sophia and looks to where his friend is dying. Noah quickly recovers himself, and just as the second wolf comes at him, he dislodges the dagger and plants it in the animal's jaw. The pair lies on the ground now, writhing, and then howling softly. Then they're dead.

Sophia has made it into the woods. She searches frantically for anything that she can use to protect herself. Finding a log, she picks it up and turns to where she thinks the attack is coming from. She sees nothing; hears nothing; just the howling of the wolves as if they are all around her. She swings into the dark, hitting nothing. Then she pauses briefly to hear that Noah is still alive.

He is! The wolves have launched a full attack on him now. Even with their dwindling numbers, he feels like he is still fighting all twelve, maybe more. A wolf rips into his forearm with its claw and blood splatters out, driving the animals crazy. Another one bites into the already gaping wound, but let's go just as soon as the dagger finds its way into its neck.

Noah keeps on retreating into the forest, needing to find Sophia, needing to make sure that she is okay, that she is safe. But he has his hands full with the animals that are charging him without letting up. He hopes that Sophia has had the sense to climb into a tree and hide. But Sophia cannot think of that. She wants to help Noah if she can just find him. She takes a few more swings in the dark and falls to the ground when she hits nothing. The wolves seem to be focusing all their attention on Noah now.

Eventually, the grunting and growling get closer, and Sophia is on her feet. She throws herself into the battle, swinging with every last ounce of energy she has. She makes contact with a wolf, in its head. It falls to the ground, and as it tries to gather itself she hits it again. She hits it until its head splits open and if it wasn't for the darkness of the night, you would see its brains.

Then she swings for another one, not missing. The

animal is large and drops to the ground with a thud. She misses twice when she tries to go for its head again, but on her third attempt split its skull open so that it too resembles its friend. Sophia has officially joined the fight.

Noah and his dagger bring down another wolf, while Sophia and her log take care of the rest. She is tired but also sick of all these delays to something she doesn't want to do anyway. It's time to get this over and done with, time to get to the Blood Baron's house and life to start, or end as it should. She brings the log down on the last wolf's head but it doesn't split. Regardless, she knows it is dead.

They look around at the carnage, at the animals that seem to be catching the moonlight now that they're dead. They keep waiting for more to appear out of the shadows, but when nothing happens for a few minutes, they both drop to the ground, exhausted.

Sophia wakes first, the sun filtering down through the trees and onto her face. She notices the deep gash on Noah's arm and tries to wake him. He responds sluggishly and she realizes that they could have a real problem. Suddenly everything is about Noah's injuries. She can't imagine losing him also, not after everything that she has lost already.

She tears the bottom half of his shirt. Leaving him alone for just a minute, she goes towards the sound of the river. Upon her return she cleans out his wound as best she can. It takes several trips to the river before she has to stop cleaning the wound. It's bleeding again. She tears a strip from the bottom of her dress off and ties it around where the blood comes out of Noah's arm. He doesn't once stir, and she is worried that he is already dead!

"Noah...Noah!" she tries to get him up. He barely

responds, just moaning. Her fear is that the wound has become infected. If only they hadn't fallen asleep. If only they had used the adrenalin that still pumped through their veins to start a fire, she might have seen the wound earlier and tended to it. She can't bear the thought of Noah dying, not like this, out here alone in the woods.

Another piece comes off her dress and she soaks it with water. She remembers the skins they have and uses the remaining water in them to wipe his face. He looks like he's gone to sleep. But it's a deep sleep, and as she wipes his brow and neck, she wonders if he will wake from it. He doesn't seem to have a fever, but it's already so hot that even if Noah was burning up, she wouldn't be able to tell. She fills the water skins and tries to get him to drink.

Noah coughs too much water in his mouth. He stirs momentarily, checking to see that she is okay. Even in his state, she is the most important thing to him in the world. Again he goes back to that place that Sophia cannot get him to come out of. All she can do is keep him cool, the trees helping somewhat.

They lose an entire day. Noah keeps slipping in and out of consciousness. He has terrible nightmares and Sophia wishes that she could go into his head and save him from the monsters chasing him. Sometimes, when he awakes, he appears to be delusional. But then he is sleeping again, Sophia cradling his head in her lap, wiping his brow and neck. Noah finally awakens just after sunset, looking remarkably rested and ready for the road.

Sophia thinks better of it. She starts a fire, her first attempt on her own, but it's easy thanks to the flint they purchased in the previous village. She checks his wound and cleans it. Her dress is now considerably shorter, more of it coming off to bandage the wound a second time. With his wound shielded tightly from the outside world, they sit down to a supper of fruit and leftover bread.

"I was afraid that you were doing to die," Sophia says, biting into an apple. She looks away so that he doesn't see the tear escaping her eye.

"You're not going to be rid of me that easily Sophia. I will always be there for you!" Noah realizes that 'always' might not be for much longer and he too turns away, not wanting Sophia to see him cry. He has fallen more in love with her on this journey. But he also knows better than to say anything about it. What good would it do either of them right now?

The pair talks for a very long time, about everything except what is truly on their minds, what really weighs heavily on their hearts. Sophia too has fallen in love with Noah. But that is inconsequential right now. Right now they must both get as much rest as is possible, thanks to Noah's injury. One more night and then they will be on their way to the Baron's house.

They haven't seen any sign of an army on the road, which is a good thing. Surely there are other routes that this army could take to get to Rowan Manor, but Sophia can only hope that this was not the case. She can only hope that her family, their lands, and all the people that trust Rowan to look after them, are safe.

She curls up to Noah, needing him. The nights are much cooler than the days, which are scorching and almost unbearable. But there can be no walking tonight, not if she is going to be sure that Noah is okay.

Noah watches her and finally lets a hand rest on her forehead. He is thankful for a lot of things, particularly that she tended to his wounds so lovingly. He is also grateful to have this time with her, a time that he would not have had, had they been back at Rowan Manor. Status and position would have kept them apart. But here, in the forest, they can pretend to be equals, even though it won't be for much longer.

"Thank you, Sophia, for everything. You might just have saved my life. And for this, I will be eternally grateful. Thank you!" He lets her catch his tears now as they fall out of his eyes and roll down his face. But he isn't weeping, not really.

Sophia wipes the tears from his face and then returns to her position, curled up tightly next to him. Noah takes her in his arms and knows that no more needs to be said now. All that he can do is watch her as she falls asleep. She must be tired from the day's efforts.

And she is. Sleep comes easily in his arms. She has come to trust him more now, more than she ever thought she would. She lets herself go completely and falls asleep in the warmth and safety of Noah's embrace.

Watching Sophia sleep Noah can't help but wonder what it would have been like had he been born into a different station in life. He wonders if he would have been allowed to pursue her, or if he would even have known of her existence, had his mother not turned up at Rowan's door all those years ago.

He sleeps easily too, finally having Sophia in his arms. This has been something that he has longed to do for a while now, but life just got in the way. He gets up occasionally to stoke the fire, needing to keep it going the whole night in case they are attacked again. Better the devil you can see!

Come morning they are both rested and ready for a full

day's walk. Despite the heat, they head off, into the clearing where they were attacked, and start the trek across it. By noon they are on the other side of it and again under the protection of the trees. The sun is relentless as it beats down upon them, but neither of them complains. They just keep walking, grateful for the occasional downpours.

As the day draws to a close they see another village in the distance and head for it. It's a much smaller village that the first and they know they must be getting closer to the Baron's compound. After making a few inquiries, they confirm that on foot, it's about a two-week journey. But should they be able to get horses, it's less than a three-day ride. After making enquiries it is clear that they will have to walk, at least to the next village. They might be able to get horses there according to the medicine woman who has a look at Noah's wound. She commends Sophia on her cleaning and management of the wound and places some herbs on it, for a fee of course. There is no inn in this village, but that's okay. Noah and Sophia feel up to walking, at least for half the night, and then they will take a break. They end up walking throughout the night, resting in the shade of a grove by the river for most of the next day.

CHAPTER 9

TWO MEN AGONIZE over Sophia now, for different reasons, and on opposite ends of the continent. Rowan worries that he has sent his daughter, his youngest, and the apple of his eye, to a life of misery. The other, the Blood Baron, wonders where she is, or if she is coming. He decides to give it a few more days before he gets an army together to go and take her from her home. He hopes secretly that it will not come to that.

Mary is inconsolable. She moves around her house in silence. Her children have left, and her grandchildren. Now it's just her and her husband, who she cannot even bring herself to speak to anymore. She tried when the girls were still here, keeping things amicable. But now there is no need to pretend any further. Rowan has given her baby away. And that is something that she cannot come to terms with, no matter what his reasons were.

She lives past her husband. He eats alone, as does she. Mary finds things to keep herself busy with, waiting for the return of Noah and Ian. At least Mary consoles herself with the fact that Sophia's lady-in-waiting, Anne, who has been with her whole life, is with her during this time. She has no idea that Ian and Anne are no more.

Rowan knows that he has wronged her. He knows that she probably will not forgive him for what he has done, and he accepts it. But that she refuses to talk to him is too much for him to take. Still, he tries, although responses from Mary are unlikely.

"Mary, we can't go on like this." He wants anything from her. He wants her to strike him and throw all manner of insults at him. Anything will be better than nothing at all. But she gives him nothing. She listens to him right enough. But she has no desire to respond to or engage with her husband in any way. She has said everything that she is going to say.

The servants have an easier time with her. Mary at least speaks to them, even if it's just to tell them what to do or to ask for something. Rowan finds himself envious of this relationship that she has with her staff now, never thinking that there would come a time when she would come to him for nothing.

He gives her her space eventually, to grieve the child that she will never see again. He can't hunt or do anything that will bring him any joy. He feels that this would not only be a slap in her face but also to the memory of Sophia. Rowan wonders often if he might have handled the whole thing differently.

At the Blood Baron's house, the situation is tense. It becomes more so with each day that Sophia does not arrive. The deadline for her delivery has been missed, and he is running out of time. He moves through the house like a lion with a thorn in his paw that he can't get out. And everyone stays out of his way, as much as they can.

Caught between planning a wedding and planning a

blood bath, the Baron is not himself. At times he is quiet and broody, and at other times he is a terror, loud and insulting. His servants really can't take it no more, but what else can they do? Work is scarce and few of them will take their chances out in the fields, heavily taxed by the people who really own them.

Everyone works fast to prepare for Sophia, despite the delay. They do it to reassure the Baron that they believe she is coming, and also to get and stay out of his way. The house teems with life every day, and everyday the Baron dies a little inside. But he will never let anybody see this.

They prepare Sophia's room on one side of the house. It's a magnificent room, and the Blood Baron is sure that she'll be very happy in it if she would just arrive. But there's still no sign of her, and everyone is worried because the Baron is getting edgy. And when he gets edgy, everybody gets nervous. He is very dangerous when he gets edgy.

Back at Rowan Manor things become unbearable for Rowan. He has given up trying to speak to his wife and spends most of his days alone in the library. He loses himself in books, finding little comfort in the pages. But at least he is well and truly out of Mary's way now.

He is also thin, losing weight as fast as he is losing hope that he will ever be reconciled with his wife. He is eating, but this brings him no joy. Even ale provides him with little comfort, so he stops drinking it altogether when it stops bringing him the numbness he desires.

The Baron inspects the preparations and is pleased. There is nothing that is out of place, except for his moods. His staff is used to his tyrannical behavior. But they still find it disconcerting when he is nice. And when he shifts between nasty and nice it is even more disconcerting, leaving them not knowing how to respond to him.

He can ill afford for them to think that he has gone soft. But as the preparations for Sophia come together he too seems to gather himself. He seems less violent, and he hasn't sent anyone to an untimely death in weeks. They hope Sophia arrives soon, hoping that she will at last bring about the change in their master that they long for.

The Baron goes to his chambers. He locks himself in after dismissing his guards. Alone, he remembers the one woman that he truly loved, the one who made him the way he is. She took his son, his only son, away, and that was too much for him to handle. He agonizes over his failed suicide, realizing that this was a moment of absolute weakness. Now, thanks to his reputation, he will replace her at last with a younger woman, one who will give him another son, the new heir to everything that he has. He cannot die before she arrives. He cannot die before he has left her with child, so that all his lands don't fall into the hands of his servants.

He looks at the bottle of hemlock and remembers that day, a year ago today. He still cannot believe that he took such a cowardly approach to this situation, and after so many years. But the truth is he did, and if his council had not found him, he would be dead. Needless to say, those council members who happened upon his dying body are! He could not stand it if word of his cowardice got out. So he did what he had to do.

He remembers his son, so perfect. He was all that the Baron ever wanted, along with his mother. But at the time, a time of war and hunger, a time of persecutions and many other tribulations, he had no other way to be. He had to be ruthless, or risk losing his land to one more ruthless than he. And he would have raised the boy to be the same way, able to stand up for himself and protect what was rightfully his. Was this so wrong?

Why did his mother have to steal him from the house so young, before he knew any better and before he could make up his own mind? Why did she have to leave, knowing the dangers that waited for her outside these walls? They must surely be dead now, it's been so long. Surely she couldn't have survived more than a few days, young as she was, with a young child in tow? This has been the Baron's agony for a very long time now, one that he hopes will be somewhat masked once his new bride arrives. He can't help but wonder though if he has not perhaps left it all too late.

He picks up the bottle of hemlock, a part of him wishing that he had taken a stronger poison, a part of him grateful that he hadn't. It's a strange thing, suicide, leaving you feeling that you had done the wrong thing even though it seemed to have been the right thing at the time, especially if you survive the attempt.

The Baron throws the bottle away, wanting to wipe away the memory of his moment of weakness. He makes sure that it will not be seen, throwing it away far from the house, having his guards wait for him a ways away as he throws the bottle into the river. He gets back to the house and locks himself away in his room, not wanting to speak to anyone, not wanting to see anyone. He will forget this.

Before long, however, his tyrannical façade has returned. He moves through the house with renewed energy, spitting vile insults at his staff, setting them all on edge again. They are again wondering what went wrong, knowing that it is nothing that they did, knowing that whatever eats away at their master is a demon that he will have to fight himself. They hope once more that Sophia will arrive soon, and that her arrival will placate the beast somewhat!

Rowan wonders at the life Sophia has now. He knows that she is a young woman of incredible resilience. But what good will her resilience be to her in the clutches of the Blood Baron? He remembers the contract, the promise that Sophia would want for nothing. If only he had shown it to his wife, and discussed it with her, then he would not be in the situation that he now finds himself in.

"She will not speak to me. She moves through the house like a ghost, a shadow. I don't know what to do. I don't know what to say. I have lost not only my little girl, but my wife also. How much can one be expected to take? Or lose? How much longer will I bear the burden of my transgression? All is lost I fear. There is no coming back from this. Sophia will forever be a void in our lives now, one that I created. We will not even see her children. I'm not sure how much longer I can stand this. Can she not see that I did this for her, for us, for everyone?" Rowan finally confides in his childhood friend and confidante, Ivan.

Ivan is a man of great wisdom. And when he notices that his friend has not been himself since his birthday, he comes back to check on him. He arrives just in time, Rowan already losing his mind from not having anyone to talk to. Even his servants seem to have sided with Mary although they don't know what is going on. Ivan breaks a long silence with his steady, measured response.

"She is a mother, Rowan. You need to understand that. You took much more than just her daughter away from her when you sent Sophia away. You took away her last chance to say goodbye to her little girl. You took away her chance to get to know her grandchildren. You took away the source of her joy in her later years. Now all she has is herself because none of the grandchildren that she does know can fill the void. She will come to loathe them, not because she wants to, but because she has to. Because anything else, loving her grandsons, will be like losing Sophia all over again. And she's French. The likelihood that she will forget this anytime soon is unlikely."

Rowan is left alone with his thoughts. He must accept that he did this. And he must accept the consequences of his actions. Ivan is right. He took much more than just a daughter from her mother, much more.

The next day he has breakfast with his friend, who has said all that he is going to say on the matter and must now leave to attend to his businesses. For the first time in a while, Rowan can eat with a semblance of a smile. Maybe it's because he actually has someone to talk to. Maybe he is just very hungry for the fresh breads that were served. They eat, and then Ivan is on his way. But before he leaves he checks in on Mary, not giving away that he knows about Sophia. He also lets Rowan know that contract or no contract, his knights are at the ready to do battle with the Blood Baron to facilitate Sophia's safe return. Rowan thanks his friend, knowing that by now Sophia must already be married to the tyrant, and probably already with a child. He watches the horses that brought his friend here disappear down through the gables and then return to the silence of his house.

Now that he understands the extent to which he has wounded his wife he doesn't attempt to speak to her. She needs time to come to terms with what has happened and then maybe one day she will come to him. But he realizes that this will take some time, probably a very long time. And this is time that he must give her if there is to be any hope of a reconciliation.

Rowan calls for his daughters. He needs his grandsons around him, for nothing else but the distraction that they will provide him. He almost regrets them, wishing that his daughters had given birth to girls. If so, then he would not be in this situation. Sophia wouldn't have been asked for, demanded, for the likelihood that she too will produce a male child.

The arrival of the children brings life to the house, except that now they have to deal with their grandmother who is not herself. But at least Mary manages to speak with them, to humor them. She takes them to the kitchen and gives them a cake. Then she sits with them around the large kitchen table, wanting to know everything about their schooling. Some of them have brought their tutors along, not knowing how long they will stay.

Rowan gathers his daughters to him, wanting to tell them everything. But he is unable to. Instead, he weaves them a tale about their mother missing her grandsons, a tale Mary does not dispute. Having their grandsons there has given Mary something else to focus on. But she still does not speak to her husband, even during dinner when the entire family, except for their sons-in-law, is gathered around the table.

Noah and Sophia are now less than two weeks away from the Blood Baron's compound. They know this from the directions they received. It's been a long and tiring journey, and they cannot wait to get there, albeit just for a bath and to sleep. Surely the Baron cannot deny them this. At least he won't deny Sophia this if the contract is anything to go by.

They read it again, together. The shade of the massive trees that are the forest that would mean that they are 'less than two day's ride from the compound' provides them with much-needed shade. Propped up against one, they go through the details of the contract.

"At least he promised that you will want for nothing," Noah breaks the silence.

"...nothing except my family, no! And what good will

having everything in the world be without my family? But I'm doing this for them. They are the most important people in my life." Sophia looks into the distance, no tears anymore. She will not cry. The time has come for her to brace herself for her new life. And she will do it with dignity, something she learned from her mother. No man must ever be privy to the struggles in a woman's heart!

So Sophia pulls herself from the place of sadness and moves the conversation along to more pleasant things. They discuss adolescence and growing up at Rowan Manor. It was the best childhood that any child could have hoped for.

"It really was wonderful, wasn't it?"

"It was, Sophia."

"Especially the summers, summer was always my favorite time at Rowan Manor." Sophia calls her father's house by its official name now, needing to distance herself from her home, and the memories that go along with it.

"Summers were the best," Noah remembers seeing Sophia mostly in the summer, when they would gather around the fountain, and in it. He remembers how nobody but Sophia would ever swim with him, because of his birthmark. He learned a lot about her from just observing her during those times. He remembers how they would sneak down to the stream, their secret swimming hole. He remembers wanting to kiss her but never having the courage to do so.

Having her within such close proximity to him, he could just lean over right now and steal a kiss. But how will this be received? Will she kiss him back, or pull away? He can't be sure, so he doesn't, watching her mouth intently now.

He notices everything about her now. The way she laughs with her mouth closed, the way she barely opens her mouth when she speaks and yet produces the fullest, richest sound, and the way she always leans towards the sun when she pauses. Watching her so closely now, just the two of them out here in the woods, everything about her is beautiful to him. She is beautiful to him.

Noah traces the outline of her perfect face. She doesn't shy away from him, instead of taking his hand and holding it to her cheek. It's a large, warm hand. He moves to her chin and pauses, then gently traces the outline of her mouth. She stops speaking, her lips quivering as his fingers glide over them, moving ever so lightly over her mouth. She opens it just enough to reveal perfect teeth.

She cups his face in both her delicate hands. She traces the outline of his strong jaw like a blind woman trying to memorize his features. She's seen his face a million times before but never touched it. Not like this. She's never really touched it this way. Sophia closes her eyes now, as much in response to his touch as to her own touching.

"Sophia..."

"No, don't Noah. Don't say it. Everything is as it should be."

"But..."

"No, don't say it!"

They are quiet now, Noah teetering on the brink of pouring his heart out to Sophia. And Sophia, knowing this, not letting him. If he reveals his feeling for her, then she would have no choice but to say how she truly feels about him. And what good will that do them, so close to the Baron's house?

Noah gently removes his hands from her face. He brings his face close to hers but doesn't kiss her. He wants to. She wants him to. But this will just say everything that she is not allowing him to say. He may just as well lay bare his chest so that she can remove his heart.

"Sophia I love you!" he finally whispers, getting the words out before they're held back in his throat. She turns away from him, not wanting to hear it.

"Sophia I need to say this. I know it won't change anything, but let me say it." He turns her face towards his again, but she looks down, not wanting to see his face, the affection in his eyes. She fears this might break her resolve to deliver herself to the Blood Baron, in which case her family will be destroyed. One love was sacrificed for another. It's the way it has to be.

Noah doesn't try to get her to look at him. He knows the battles she fights inside and he won't make it any harder for her. But he needs to say what's been weighing on his heart and then he will be done with it. He needs to get it out before it completely destroys him.

Back at the Baron's house he too has another problem, one that he has kept even from his closest generals. He locks himself away in his room with his physician, who has come to him disguised as a nobleman from far off. He cannot let anyone know that in the last battle he took a sword to his side, an injury he has been hiding from his staff in case they got any ideas.

"It's bad Baron, and there might not be much that I can do to continue to help you, especially if you don't rest." The physician doesn't fear him as others do, knowing that he is needed here.

"Just do what you can man, keep me alive a little while longer." The Baron is desperate.

"I can give you something for the pain, again. But your constant movements make it difficult for the wound to get back together, and it's going to be hard enough keeping the infection out."

"Just do what you can."

Without the morphine, the Baron finds it difficult to move. But the movement is essential if he is to keep up this farce. He needs to be well enough when Sophia gets here, so that he can marry her, and they can consummate their marriage. Once, maybe twice and she will be with child. He needs a male heir to replace the one that was stolen from him.

He is told how much morphine to take, just enough to make movement bearable. He takes some now, and has to restrain himself from drinking the whole bottle for the severity of his injury. He will make it, just until Sophia arrives.

"Where is she?" he asks the physician as he packs up his things, preparing to leave.

"She will be here Baron. Of this I am sure. Nobody would dare to go against you, not even in your current state." The physician realizes too late that he should not have added the second part to his statement. "She will be here," he says, and takes his leave.

Noah and Sophia are sitting quietly less than two days ride from his compound and he doesn't know this. But it's about a two week walk, with hills and valleys and a road that would cut the journey in half if it didn't circle so many times. But nobody ever goes to the Baron's compound on foot. How is he to know that the woods just beyond the hills hide his bride? And how can Noah and Sophia know that they will get no horses or help in the next village so that they have to walk the entire way?

CHAPTER 10

WITH THE TIME pressing on them now, they release each other to the fates. Destiny can be kind. But she can be cruel too. And she is proving herself to be most cruel indeed when it comes to Noah and Sophia.

"Sophia wake up." Noah wakes her around midnight. He has decided that they need to get on the road so that they can be traveling before the sun is at its peak the next day. They will walk for at least twelve hours at a time now, Noah is also anxious to get to where they need to be.

He feels like he's lost Sophia already. And for all intents and purposes, he has. She has an absolute resolve now, one that he cannot break. Noah would like to drag out the last two weeks he has with her, but he knows that he would just be prolonging the inevitable. They just need to get to the Blood Baron. He needs to hand her over and then begin the long journey home. He thinks of what waits for him upon his return, no longer concerned for their destination.

He remembers his mother, and the admonition she gave him when he left. 'Be safe, come back!' He intends to do just that now. Once he has delivered Sophia safely to her new home, he will return.

They get to a hamlet, a few loosely connected houses that can't really be called a village. They're told that there will be no civilization again before they get to the Blood Baron. Again they are advised to turn back, that going on would be a traumatic experience, especially for one as delicate as Sophia. With the road they've already traveled, she still appears as soft as ever. Although Noah knows better.

Noah manages to get them provisions for three days. Anything longer would spoil. They are assured however that there is plenty of game, rabbits and such, quails and pigeons, between their little homesteads and the Baron's compound. So at least they won't starve. The river also runs through the Baron's compound, so they will not go thirsty. They just need to keep the river in sight, except for the two days they're told that it will disappear from sight because of the road they will be traveling.

They are grateful for the help they receive. Noah will probably pass this way again upon his return but still he greets the people like he will never see them again. Sophia will never see them again, and she hugs the man who let them take fruit from his sparse store, knowing this.

They did not exaggerate the treacherous terrain, although both Noah and Sophia had hoped that they had in their efforts to get them to turn back. The hills are steep, and the path allows for just one horse to pass through at a time. Two people on foot are a bit more forgiving, but Noah has to lead the way, providing Sophia with the aid she needs to assail the hills. They veer off the path to get water often, the blazing sun demanding it. They walk throughout the day, not seeing a place where they can rest up, no trees, and therefore no shade.

The Baron's compound is on such a hill, with a vantage point of seeing at least two days' ride in all directions. It is a fortress that comes into view in the far distance often as the pair travels, one that provides them with both relief, and incredible sadness. Now they know for sure where they are going, and if it wasn't for the hills, if not for the regular trips off the path down to the river to replenish their skins, they could get there much quicker. There is also the small matter of sleep. And come nightfall that is all they want to do, even if it's just for a few hours.

They curl up in the pocket between two hills. The bag serves as a pillow for Sophia, no longer able to bring herself to lie in Noah's arms. He lets her get comfortable before he chooses his resting place. But sleep doesn't come easily for him.

He cannot imagine, try as he might, a life without Sophia. The thought pains him, physically, so that he cannot sleep. He wonders how he will cope at Rowan Manor without her, even if his mother is there. He cannot think that he will forever be in the employ of Rowan, although he's been nothing but good to them. He thinks that when his mother can no longer perform her duties as a seamstress, he will take her away from there, and try his hand at being a blacksmith. Again his thoughts turn to Sophia, sleeping from exhaustion and not because she doesn't want to speak to him, and again it is as though a dagger has sliced through his gut.

So this is what love feels like. It hurts, like hell. Noah scouts their periphery one last time before he turns to face the other way and tries to sleep. It does not come, and soon they have to be up again when the moon is high enough in the sky to light their way. Gently he wakes Sophia, and again they are on their way.

They don't speak to one another by the time the sun comes up. Sweat falls off them like running water. When the road appears to go away without suddenly rising into a steep inclination there is a brief reprieve. But no sooner have they become comfortable walking along a somewhat straight road, Noah is again giving Sophia a very sweaty hand up a very steep hill.

"Wait, I can't..." Sophia is truly exhausted. She too wishes now that she had turned back at the hamlet. She wonders at how Ian would have got them to the Baron's compound in a carriage. She remembers Anne. There must be another way to get there, but they just don't have the time to find it. They press on through the heat, not feeling it anymore except for when they stop for water. The sun seems to get at them most when they're standing still.

Noah pulls her along for the better part of the day, going slowly every time she wants to stop. The fortress-like compound comes into view again, and it appears to be so close. But then they look at where the earth rises and lowers in-between, and they understand why it is a two-week journey.

"Come on Sophia, just a little bit more, please. We will rest soon, I promise." Noah is already looking around for a place for them to eat and rest up. Thankfully the sun moves across the sky so that it casts shadows in the wake of the hills. So they move from shade to sun repeatedly but don't stop. Eventually, as the sun sets, they find a perch on a hill from which they can see the river and the compound. It's rocky, but Noah feels safer in it than he did in the dip the previous night.

Sophia falls to the ground. She wants to throw herself in the river just to cool down but it seems too far. Without thinking she pours the remaining water from her skin over herself and then perches up against a rock. She looks at Noah, who is selecting fruits for their dinner, and imagines what lies ahead for her.

"Do you think he's really as bad as everybody says?" she asks, pointing in the general direction of the compound with her head.

"Everybody can't be wrong about him, so yes, I think he is as bad as everyone says he is." Noah's response is candid but honest.

Noah pulls her to him, disregarding dinner. Her back settles into his chest comfortably. Their faces touch.

"He'll be different with you I'm sure. He wouldn't have asked for you if he didn't love you." Noah is clutching at straws, not sure what to say to make Sophia feel better, less anxious.

"But how can he know me? How is it possible for a man I've never met to love me?" Sophia questions this for the first time really. She doesn't understand. "Unless my father..." She stops herself, not wanting to believe anything bad about her father. It's enough that she won't see him again. Or her mother...

"You are very easy to love Sophia." Again Noah crosses an imaginary line that neither of them has drawn.

He turns her face to his. Gently he plants a kiss on her forehead. Sophia's eyes close as she takes everything about the moment. She cannot pull away from him, given their position, but she doesn't want to either. Then he kisses her nose and she giggles. Noah leaves his lips planted on the soft flesh. Sophia is everything that he has ever allowed himself to believe she was. His eyes close briefly as they breathe each other in.

Shaking, he lets go of her nose with his lips. He looks at her mouth for the longest time. Then he looks deep into her eyes, a look that she doesn't turn away from. Every part of her wants him to kiss her, every part of him wanting nothing else. They stare at each other for an eternity.

Then, slowly, he goes for her mouth with his. He needs to be sure that this is what she wants. As their lips touch they both warm up considerably. The air is cooling in the night, but Noah and Sophia are on fire. He holds her head now, keeping her firmly in place so that he can complete the kiss. She has no intention but to let anything but that happen. She lets him support her head as their lips lock, her knees going weak so that she is grateful that they are sitting down.

They pull away from each other just before the passion overtakes them. Gazing at each other longingly, Noah wants nothing more than to put his lips on her again. But he fears that he may not be able to stop a second time. He gets up and goes and gets their dinner. They eat in relative silence before Sophia takes the bag and places it under her head. She looks away from him as he watches her, knowing that she isn't sleeping, but not knowing what to say to her.

When sleep finally comes, they sleep the entire night. At dawn, Sophia is woken up by a butterfly flittering around her face. She gets up slowly, not wanting to disturb it.

"Noah," she whispers. "Noah, wake up."

Noah wakes to the sight of the butterfly on her fingers. They stare at it as it dances over her hand and then flies off. They pack up and head out, in silence for the most part. Both of them cannot get last night out of their minds. And both of them go to places with it that they would otherwise not allow themselves to go.

Rowan has taken the boys fishing. They love it. Some of

them are knee-deep in the river, scaring the fish away. But this trip isn't about catching anything. He just wants to get out of the house, away from his silent wife, and away from the looks, he is getting from his daughters.

The whole world seems to be against him now, except for the boys. All they know is that they are spending time with their grandfather, and that to them is priceless. They are not aware of the rift that has grown between their grandparents, getting adequate attention from both of them.

Laurel, Rowan's eldest daughter, comes to find them and watches for a moment the incredible bond between a grandfather and his grandsons. She wonders what it would be like if they had all given birth to girls. She wonders what the addition of a girl to the mix would do. But this is not the reason that she has come to find Rowan, alone, and away from the house.

"Father..." she almost whispers, not wanting to disturb the children at play, some of them taking the fishing very seriously.

"Laurel, my child. Come!" Rowan calls her to him, happy that someone has finally broken the stalemate. "Sit, sit..." He moves along somewhat on the log that is his chair. She gathers her dress and sits down next to her father.

Laurel takes her father's hand and looks closely at it, how thin it is. She looks at his face, withered and weathered. How thin he's become.

"What's the matter father...what is going on between you and mother? This isn't normal, it isn't right." She speaks with a softness that makes Rowan want to tell her everything.

"Nothing child. There is no problem." Even as the words come out he doesn't believe them. How could he possibly think that she would?

"But father, we all see how you live past each other, not speaking to one another. What is the matter? And why are we here? Please father, the truth!" Again her tone is soft, not accusing. Rowan appreciates this, particularly because everyone in the house thinks that he is the problem. He accepts that he is, but the way Laurel speaks with him almost consoles him. But he doesn't feel he has the courage yet to tell her the truth.

"We just missed you, that is all. You worry too much child. And besides, the disagreements of parents should never affect their children, no matter how old they are." He cracks a smile, taking her hand in his now and putting his forehead to hers, wishing that the thoughts in his head could magically be transferred to her so that he doesn't have to say anything. Then she can go about the business of hating him, as his wife does, and they can get back to the place where he is an outsider in his own home.

"So there has been a disagreement between you?!" She digs further, wanting to know what could possibly have caused her parents, who have loved each other since she can remember, even before, to drift so horribly apart.

"Yes my child, there has been a falling out. But we will get passed this soon, and then you can be on your way, back to your husbands, back to your lives." His answer does little to reassure Laurel, who now knows that they have been sent for the purpose of bridging the gap between their parents. But how can they, when they don't know what the problem is?

"Don't worry Laurel, everything will be fine." Rowan tries to sound more reassuring this time. Even though he knows that things will never be alright again. He has lost Sophia forever, sent her away to a life unknown, and nobody but his wife and best friend knows this. Ian and

Anne are dead-something he does not know and he gave express instructions to Ian that Noah was to wait outside. When his daughters find out, life will become an unbearable burden for him, and he will lose them all. This is a loss that he cannot face.

On the third day, the path meanders close to the river, and Noah is relieved. It's sunset, and he tosses the backpack to the ground. Then, with a splash, he disappears beneath the cool water. He comes up, inviting Sophia in, but she just soaks her feet in the cold water. She cannot wet her dress, and they're a little too old to be swimming naked together.

Again he disappears beneath the waters. He stays under a little too long, Sophia worried now. She calls for him, but there is no response.

"Noah, this isn't funny." Her voice is a mixture of stern disapproval and concern. Still, he remains underneath the water. She wades in slowly until she is waist-deep in the river when suddenly he appears right in front of her. She gives him a dirty look laced with relief.

Then they are both under the water, the coolness of it inviting. For a moment all is forgotten and they remember their swimming hole back at Rowan Manor. They remember the many summer days spent in it alone when life was simple and they knew what to expect. How did things get so complicated?

Back on dry land, Noah starts a fire. He wonders if somewhere in the distance, at the Baron's house, he isn't looking down at them right now, the smoke from the fire rising quickly. He doesn't mind this, at least knowing that he will know that they are coming. The pain of losing Sophia forever cuts into him again.

"Come closer to the fire," he beckons. She comes as close as she can without burning herself. She wishes she had got another dress, the one she has on so wet now that it seems like it will be impossible for the whole thing to dry. Sophia turns around, slowly, like a beautiful gazelle on a spit. He sits, shirtless, and watches her almost dancing herself dry.

"You're beautiful." The words come out louder than he may have liked.

"Thank you," comes the response. She is thanking him for everything he has done for her, and not just for the compliment.

He pulls the backpack to him to reveal the remainder of their provisions. Some apples, and cheese. It's all they have left but it will have to do for dinner. He tosses an apple at her, practically through the flames, and she catches it with both hands. She smiles at him before taking a bite, not really hungry, but knowing that she needs to eat. She continues her dance, the flames licking the skirt of the modest dress, torn from where she had to get bandages for Noah's wound. She looks at his arm, still bandaged, the herbs still at work, or what's left of them. "Thank you, Noah," she says.

"Did you ever think of me, like that, back at Rowan Manor?" he asks, not sure why he feels the need to know this now.

"Like what?" Sophia avoids answering the question by throwing another at him. Of course, she thought of him 'like that'.

"You know what I mean. Like that!" He adds an element of cheek to his response, just in case she says no.

"All the time, Noah. I thought of you 'like that' all the time." Her response makes it difficult for him to swallow the piece of cheese in his mouth.

"Then why did you not say anything?" He really wants to know now, why she waited until she knew they could not be together to express anything other than friendship towards him.

"Protocol, my dear Noah. It was not my place to discuss such things with you. You had to approach my father and request permission to court me before I started making such proclamations." Again he is reminded of their different stations, and he wonders if he might have had the guts to do so.

He lets her words sit with him for a while, as he finishes what's left of the cheese, Sophia not wanting any more. She has her back to the flames now, needing to dry that part of her dress before she sits down. He moves in behind her, not thinking.

"Noah, the dress has to dry or I'll catch a cold. You wouldn't want your precious cargo to arrive any more disheveled than she already is, would you?"

He doesn't move, tracing the outline of both her shoulders at the same time. Noah is consumed with passion now, wanting to be with Sophia, wanting to give her an experience she has never had, one that can linger long after they are no more together. He wants her to feel true love before he delivers her to a man who can never, will never, love her the way he does.

"Let's just forget where we are, and why, just for tonight, please. Let me love you, Sophia, let me make love to you."

This is so unexpected that she giggles before she catches herself, realizing that he is serious. "Please," he continues to beg.

"But I've never been with a man, Noah, and..." He knows this. And he knows that she is concerned for her virginity, which wasn't in the contract but assumed to be implied, her being Rowan's youngest daughter, and all of them being virtuous.

"I just want to know you for one night, to know the fullness of your passions, uninhibited, for one night. Then I can live out the rest of my days knowing that I loved you, but once. Please!"

She turns to face him, and before she can speak he kisses her. It's a deep, sweet kiss, laced with apple and cheese. She loves it. Her mouth opens to receive his tongue and he lets it slide inside, between her teeth, and find hers. Their tongues dance around each other, inside her mouth, then his. Their lips join together in a way that can only be described as magic.

Sophia pulls away. She walks down to the river, her feet in the water. She wishes she could just throw herself into it, to diffuse the fire that Noah has started in her, and never to resurface. She wants to be lost forever to this world now that she cannot have, truly have, the man that she loves.

He follows her, and they watch the water rushing over their feet. He puts out his hand for her to take. She takes it. They make their way back to the fire, its warmth reaching them long before they get there. Sophia is conflicted now more than ever, but what she does know, is that she wants Noah to kiss her again.

He does, making sure that he has her well in hand as her knees give way again. He eases them to the ground where they lie in the soft grass, side by side. He kisses her with a passion and fury of a man possessed. She kisses him back the same way. If only she knew that he too, for all his sudden confidence, has never been with a woman this way. It will be a first for both of them, and probably a last.

Noah is on top of Sophia now, but she can't even feel his weight. She is lost in the beauty of the moment, the one-time-onlyness of it all. If the Baron wants a virgin, she will not be one. She lets herself go to Noah knowing that by the time this night is over, she won't be a virgin anymore.

Noah undresses first, so that Sophia is not as insecure about herself. She has nothing to be insecure about mind you. She is perfect in every way, right down to the beauty spot right next to her naval. She allows him to take her dress off, and her underclothes. Naked now, they return to kissing, fueling the fire that will lead them down the path of lovemaking.

Noah fumbles for a minute. He has no experience to draw from, no reference for what he is doing. All he knows is that he wants to do it, with all his heart, and with every fiber of his being. Sophia doesn't even notice this, not knowing what to expect. She just knows that when Noah gets to the place he so desperately wants to be, it will be wonderful.

They continue to kiss, Noah moving his hands all over her delicate little body, wanting to feel every part of her at once. She has completely surrendered to him now, trusting that he will take them where they need to be. And he wants to be everywhere.

He pauses for a moment, finding that place between her thighs where many men have longed to be. He takes her, completely, and she tenses up, a mild pain in her groin that she knows, thanks to Anne, will go away shortly. It does, and they proceed to make the most beautiful love. Noah is patient and loving, kindness dripping from him along with the sweat now. She doesn't close her eyes, watching his face. His eyes are on her too, grateful, hungry, passionate eyes. This is love.

They make love over and over again, not getting their fill of one another, drowning in their ecstasies. She receives him into her repeatedly, wanting him back there every time he is not. Noah wants her as badly, and there is nothing now that separates them, nothing keeps them apart.

The night seems to drag on as they remain wrapped in one another. If she is never going to experience this kind of love again, then she will make sure that she remembers this night. Noah wants nothing else for her, but that she remembers him as her first. Thoughts of the Baron and what lies ahead disappear as they dive once more into the river of sensual ecstasy that neither of them had planned.

Noah wraps his arms around her now, wanting to keep her safe and warm. They have had their fill of love for the night. He says nothing, and she says nothing. Not because they're embarrassed or ashamed, but because there is nothing left that they can say with their mouths that hasn't been said with their bodies. They fall asleep under a clear, star-filled sky, and Noah knows that he will never love another again the way he has loved here tonight. Sophia knows the same thing.

They make love again in the morning, just before dawn, and the morning sun finds them wrapped in one another again. Then they dive into the river, colder from the night, and try to clean up without washing each other off of them. All is not well for Sophia and Noah, they know this. But they know that no matter what, they will forever have last night, and they will forever have this morning.

They head out, a spring in both their steps that belies their destination. But who cares for such things right now? Who worries, when there has been love shared? They're grateful that they didn't find any horses in the previous village, grateful for a lot of things. But mostly they are grateful for each other.

The journey ahead is the most dangerous. The river

will disappear for two days from sight and so they make sure their skins are full. They pace themselves, drinking only when absolutely necessary, and even then just a sip. Noah sets traps for quail and rabbits, which are aplenty as they were told at the previous village. He catches a rabbit, and this will be their dinner tonight. Breakfast and lunch are impossible to even think of in the heat!

CHAPTER 11

NOAH AND SOPHIA cannot control themselves anymore. No sooner have they stopped to rest for the day than they are consumed by each other, unable to hold back. The setting sun now finds the two making love, and they make love for most of the night. They even forget to eat, needing to, but not wanting to waste time with the preparation of food, not when they can be making love!

When they are not making love they are sleeping, briefly, dreaming of a life that could have been. Both of them wonder what it would be like to be able to live this way forever, just loving each other, and making love to one, with one another.

They know how this will end though, how it must end. But none of them mentions it anymore. Thinking about it is too painful. And this is a pain that they can both do without, at least for the remainder of their journey.

Noah wonders if he was a knight in Rowan's court, would it have been more acceptable for him to court Lady Sophia. He imagines going off to battle, perhaps even against the Blood Baron, and returning victorious, Sophia waiting for him. He hates Rowan for not letting them all know what the Blood Baron wanted, for not giving them an opportunity to fight for Sophia, for not giving him the opportunity to fight for her.

He doesn't say this, but he hates Rowan for this most of all; for not giving them a choice in a matter so important, so significant. But why would he? It's not like Noah is of any bloodline blue enough to warrant this. He hates that he isn't. He continues to hate Rowan silently for giving in so easily.

Sophia doesn't think of this. She just appreciates this time that she has with Noah, and appreciates the turn things have taken. She wants to be with him forever but is grateful for the time she has with him. She has made peace with the way things will end. And so she focuses on just milking every moment she has left with Noah.

Reality keeps biting them though, and both of them are silent at these times. Fortunately, it happens at the same time, neither questioning the other's silence. They know what it means and just let it go.

All they can do now is make every second count. They hunt together, prepare supper together, and when the river reappears as if by magic, they swim together, even making love in the water. It is the best time of their lives and neither of them will forget it. It will make Sophia's new home more bearable, knowing that she had this time with Noah. And it will make the rest of Noah's life more bearable, the memories of this time.

The landscape starts to change and they know they are getting close. Less than a week away from the Baron's house now, they become heavier and heavier with the burden of what they are about to lose. They both contemplate slowing down, stopping even, but none of them says anything. They press on, the lovemaking becoming more intense as they approach.

It's an amazing thing about impending loss. It makes you more appreciative of what you have, even though you had it right in front of you your whole life. The days seem to go quickly now, and the pair becomes more withdrawn from one another, except when they make love that is.

The Baron is now convinced that Sophia is not coming. He calls his generals to him, reluctantly. But he has no choice. She is a woman who is young enough to raise a child, and it is almost guaranteed that she will give him a boy. He really has to get to her and get her to come to him.

"I will not be going with you. I have business to take care of here, and I cannot hand it over to anybody." He is referring to his injury, but doesn't say it. "Gather some men, and storm Rowan Manor. No need for killing. But do what you must to ensure that you return with her. Now go, quickly!"

They leave him alone, going to get ready to do battle if needs be, for Sophia. He has been unable to stand throughout. The pain is unbearable, and his worst fear is being realized. The wound is becoming infected, and without rest, proper rest, he will not survive to welcome Sophia, even with the army that he has sent to get her.

The morphine helps him to stand. He makes it to his room and closes the door. He falls into the bed, desperate for the physician to return now, to make this pain go away. He is an old man, and his body doesn't heal as quickly as it used to. But he just needs Sophia to get here, where he hopes he will be able to consummate their union and leave her with a child.

His servants notice that he is taking strain, that movement is difficult. But they know that the worst thing they can ask him is 'how are you today?" So they don't.

It takes two days for the army to get organized. He makes it to the front door, to see them off. They are bloodthirsty barbarians, so for him to admonish them against killing is pointless. They will find a reason to shed blood. He cannot worry about this right now. He will not know the extent of the damage that they have done anyway. Sophia will be here, and that is all that matters.

Rowan has also been anxious over the last while. Ian and Noah were supposed to be back by now. He looks out of the window of one of the guest bedrooms in his house, a room that is essentially his for the foreseeable future. He wonders where they might be, hoping that everything went well.

"Father..." Laurel is still the only one speaking to him. "What's wrong?"

"Nothing child, just thinking, that is all!" Again he knows that she could not possibly believe him, him not believing himself.

She lets it go. "Dinner is ready father, will you come to sit with us?" She is really trying to get to the bottom of things with her parents, knowing that they cannot leave it like this. And their children, whose lives have been disrupted by this, are the ones who are suffering, even though the boys won't say this.

"Yes dear, let's go." He takes her hand and they go downstairs to the massive dining room. She puts her father at his seat at the head of the table, filling all the other chairs with her sisters so that their mother has to sit next to him. It's a start.

She can only hope that one of them will break soon and

that this silence will be over. The only conversation at the table is between them and their mother, or them and their father, but not all of them together. This is a most unpleasant situation indeed, one that will soon be evident to the older children.

Sophia and Noah are less than four days away from the compound now, but the Baron doesn't know. They are anxious now to the point that lovemaking is no longer possible. They just lay in each others arms, knowing that in a few days their lives will forever and irreparably be changed.

"We're almost there now." Noah states the obvious. He is unable to avoid the inevitable now, wanting once more to take Sophia far away from this whole situation and pretend it isn't happening.

"Almost..." Sophia knows this, but she doesn't want to hear it. She too wishes that she could just disappear, but knowing that she can't.

"I thank you for this time that you have given me. I thank you for giving yourself to me. I thank you for..."

"Noah...it was my pleasure." She answers him with a certainty that belies their situation. In four days she will be left alone to face a new life, without even Anne, who has been her confidante since she can remember, by her side. "I look terrible though, he might just turn me away." She tries to add humor to the situation. It doesn't work.

No more talking now as they press on, through the night. No talk of home, or their childhood, or the last couple of days. He just helps her over hills and around them, she just takes his hand quietly and lifts herself over the hills, and over the rocks at the base of the hills. The silence between them is not uncomfortable. But it is unsettling!

The army sets out two days later. The men in it are fierce, ready for action. They are divided into four battalions, a hundred strong each. There is no need for any more, according to the Baron. Rowan has less than fifty knights in his fold, and four hundred men versus fifty is no competition. He is sure that they will return with his woman.

He watches them as they take off, making haste through the gates to his compound. He is confident of this, but at what cost? The Baron watches as the last of the horses disappears through the gate, the massive gates closing, and hopes that they just get back in time.

Instead of going back into the house, he staggers into his garden. He looks at the summer blossoms in full bloom and wonders if Sophia will like them. He is trying to convince himself that this is a courtship, a real relationship. He remembers the beginnings of this garden, and who started it.

She planned it meticulously and then tended it with as much care. He hardly remembers what the expanse looked like before. He hadn't even believed that it was arable. But she proved him wrong. She always had a way of proving him wrong.

If only he had made her his wife. But those were different times, and he had a bevy of concubines. If he had made an honest woman of her, she might not have taken her child and run.

But it's too late to think of such things, too late for hopes and dreams. He can now only hope that the new woman in his life, his short life if the infection is anything to go by, will appreciate it as much. He plucks a blossom, smells it while looking around to see that no one sees him, and then drops it to the ground.

He struggles up the steps that will get him in his back door. He pauses, looking around to see what he has done here, what has been achieved. For all this to fall into the hands of servants, servants who will probably fight over it and break it apart, sharing the spoils amongst themselves, is too much for him to bear.

Noah and Sophia are once again lost in one another, the last time. He moves his hands over her, trying to remember every part of her. He looks at her in the moonlight, how she seems to absorb all the colors of the moon. And then he kisses her, long and deep, like he will never have the chance to do it again.

She gives herself to him now more than any of the other times. Sophia lets Noah have all of her, not wanting there to be anything left for the Baron, no part of her that he can own. And Noah takes it all, willingly, possessively even.

They lay naked in each other's arms, Noah still moving his fingers up and down the length of Sophia. Both of them know that this is the last time that they will make love. The rest of the journey will need all their strength if they are to make it to the forest that lines two sides of the compound.

"This was beautiful..." Noah!

"Brief, but beautiful..." Sophia!

They fall asleep, naked, with no care for any clothing since they are safely tucked away in a dip, the last one before the road suddenly spreads wide and opens up, leading them directly to the Baron's front gate. It's a long stretch of road, but at least there are no more hills to meander over, no more valleys. Both of them sleep comfortably, not knowing anything, yet knowing everything. They have made that last transition into adulthood. And they are grateful that they did this with each other.

The earth starts to shake under them, and they are stirred. It's the middle of the night, and when they wake, they're freezing. Noah gets his pants on, then his shirt. Sophia struggles with her dress so that he has to help her with it. They listen to where the sound of a million horses galloping towards them is coming from.

Noah is happy in their hiding place, certain that they cannot be seen. But they have the vantage of seeing everything that is coming towards them now. And by the light of the moon, an army comes into view. Sophia's heart beats a little faster.

"What are we going to do Noah? They're headed for..."

"We don't know that for sure. Let me think."

He takes too long to think, and one hundred horses go by, lifting dust high into the night sky. Then two hundred, the dust a constant cloud now. Soon all four hundred horses have gone by them, making their way to where the path narrows considerably so that only one horse can pass through at a time. They have to get to the Baron's quickly now so that he can get a messenger to the army for them to stop, to turn back.

Suddenly it all becomes very real for Sophia. Everything that she heard about the Baron circles in her head, as though there are a million voices speaking at once. Her stomach turns, but she grabs Noah's hand and pulls him along. They really need to get there now.

Sophia is practically running, grateful suddenly for the missing part of her dress so that her ankles are free to move. She doesn't even look back to check that Noah is following. She disappears around a bend, Noah having to stop, his wound aching and threatening to split open again.

When he finds her she has made it to the tree line. She is half bent over, one hand on a tree as she tries to catch her breath. He comes up behind her and stops, needing to catch his breath too.

"Sophia, we'll get there. It will be alright." He says this while thinking of his mother back at Rowan Manor. But his arm really hurts so that they have to walk, albeit quickly. The forest they're in seems to be tended to by gardeners. It's a wonderland of trees that Sophia hasn't seen before. And as the sun comes up and spreads its rays through the leaves, she feels like she is dreaming. It's beautiful. So beautiful in fact that she has to stop, just to soak it all in. This might be the last she sees of this, and she really takes it all in.

The army has come to a practical standstill now. One by one the horses take on the path. This is the shortest way to Rowan Manor, but the path is inconvenient, to say the least. The sun has already started its ascent into the sky and they are suffering. But the prospect of a bloodbath is one that they find too appetizing to pass up. They keep moving, stopping only to drink their horses and themselves.

They arrive at the hamlet and shoot through it like the arrows of an expert archer. Soon they will be at the first real village, where they will stop and eat. They also have the idea of resting for the better part of the day, and traveling at night when it's cooler. This buys Sophia and Noah the time they need.

Moving through the woods they are both practically running now. They need to get to the Baron's compound before the army gets to Rowan Manor. And they will. But they can't be sure that the Baron is even home. They assume that he is leading the army that will descend upon Rowan Manor in a few days.

When night falls it feels like they have been running the whole day. Sophia stumbles to the ground, unable to move. She drags herself up against a tree, her head between her legs. Noah stops and turns to see her on the ground. He goes to her and sits next to her without touching her. They can hardly breathe now, so they take the minute necessary for them to compose themselves.

When they do, no words come to them, they're unable to speak. They want to keep going but can't, needing to rest. The animals gather around them, curious at the pair. They are too tired to notice. And if they were to be attacked by wolves tonight, they would not be able to put up a fight.

Sleep on Sophia's last free night comes easy, thanks to all the running. Noah too sleeps remarkably well, despite what the next day has in store for them. If the Baron is not at the compound, and if they are not received, this would be very bad for their families back home. How will they make anyone believe that she is indeed Sophia, given her current state?

The sun rises and they sleep through it for the first time. Noah wakes first. Sophia wakes only when the pain in her legs becomes unbearable. She has no choice but to be alert and aware of it. It feels like she is continuously being stabbed with a thousand daggers, relentlessly.

She doesn't scream, taking it silently, not wanting to give this away. But Noah notices her struggling even to sit up. It's because she pushed herself too hard the day before, nerves getting the better of her. But she doesn't regret the pain, her love for her family fueling her on until she just couldn't anymore, physically.

Noah lifts her up. She resists for a moment until she realizes that this is futile. Even with his injured arm, he carries her easily. She throws her arms around him, not expecting him to carry her too far, but needing to give him the satisfaction. He manages to carry her for half the day.

By the time he puts her down, she has managed to get

some of the feeling back in her legs. They rest up briefly. And then slowly make their way over the last stretch, the forest suddenly giving way to the road again. It leads straight up to the massive front gates to the compound, gates that Noah and Sophia can now see.

Turning back is now out of the question. They have to get to these gates, and they have to be let in. The army will have made some considerable headway by now, but Noah and Sophia know that this is not so much that they cannot be stopped by a single messenger, one that will not be too inhibited by the narrowing path.

They hold hands for a while, and then they stop. They stare at one another and then embrace. Noah holds Sophia to him tightly, wanting to remember this moment, wanting to remember everything about her and this moment. She embraces him, knowing that when she lets him go, she will let her dreams of the life that almost was going as well. They just hold each other tightly for a long time.

Then they continue walking, the gates getting bigger and bigger as they approach them. It seems almost like they will be swallowed up by the gates, long before they even arrive, and then the gates will spit just one of them out, Noah, who must make the journey back, alone now.

Noah walks in front of Sophia, her legs not giving her as much of a problem as earlier, but just in case they are not received well. He is prepared to fight anyone that will do her harm, but he knows that this is a fight that he is going to lose eventually.

The army in the meantime has rested for most of the day and is preparing to ride out again. They mount their horses, water skins filled, and make for Rowan Manor. Three more villages stand between them and the place they intend turning into a bloodbath. They stick to the road, knowing that this is the shortest route between them and battle. They're ready to do battle.

Back at the compound, the Baron takes some more morphine, as much to drown out the pain as to drown out the thought of Sophia's entire family being eliminated. He cannot think of this, wanting to just sleep and wake when she is here. But the anxiety of it all makes this impossible.

He moves through his house in a semi-haze, not sure what he wants. He gets to Sophia's room and looks into it, examining everything, trying to find mistakes but also appreciating the work that has gone into it. He really is a much changed man deep inside. He's been changing since the day his son was taken from him.

He really struggles now to get back to his own bedroom, stopping at every window along the way to look out over the front of his house. The prettiness of it all takes him aback, and he realizes that he never truly appreciated it while he yet had years in him. He regrets this now, wishing that he had taken more time to truly appreciate what he had, instead of terrorizing people.

But he was angry. And deep anger, unabated, comes out in a very many ways. He would plunder whole villages, wage war with people who really had no fight with him, just because he was angry. But this anger has gotten him nowhere. And now, in this massive house, alone, he knows that it was not worth it. He sacrificed people for things, and that has left him an old man inside and out, an old man with nobody but the walls for company. He has no friends, no true friends, and his servants fear him. He wonders if it has all been worth it, knowing the answer to this even before the question has completely formed in his mind!

Rowan Manor is quiet now. The boys are all taking a much-needed nap after their afternoon ride with their grandfather. Rowan is starting to show signs of recovery as if he has been ill for a long time and the cure for his condition has just been discovered. This cure will leave his house soon.

Laurel sits with her father in his library, going through the books on the shelves but not taking one in particular. She has something to say to her father that he will not like, but she needs to say it nonetheless.

"We're leaving in a few days..." She lets the words hang in the air like the chandelier, not expecting him to respond. She just says it and leaves it.

"When are you planning to take your leave from us," he asks her, smiling; a forced smile, but smiling nonetheless.

"In the next two or three days. It's just that the boys need to return to the schedules, and our husbands are probably starting to wonder..."

Rowan understands. He has to. He has kept them here too long already. But he appreciates that he will have a few more days with his grandsons.

Noah and Sophia push the last stretch up to the enormous gates. Suddenly the nerves return. Sophia runs her fingers over the gate, along its walls. She wonders once more at the life she left behind, and at what awaits her just beyond these gates.

"So this is it?"

"This is it!"

Noah wants to take her in his arms but holds himself back. He just looks into her eyes as they catch the last rays of the sun. He really has no idea how he is going to deal with his life henceforth. Sophia also has no clue, but this is something that she has to do. She just has to.

The moment seems suspended, both of them having a lifetime of things that they wish they had said to each other, but can't. They have arrived, and it's time to cross over to the unknown. Sophia takes the massive knocker in hand, and then replaces it, unable to do what she must. Noah steps forward and takes it in his hands. He too doesn't yet have the courage to let her go completely.

"Maybe we should fix our appearance a little." She says this while pulling her hair into a high bun that reveals the outline of the most delicate cheeks. Using nothing but her hair she secures it. Noah wants to touch her, but he knows that he can never touch her again like that.

He straightens his shirt, not making much of a difference to their appearance. They check the bag for the contract, and Noah places the dagger back inside it. It will do him no good on the other side of these walls.

They look at one another for the last time. And then they knock, together. After the longest time, it seems they have not been heard, so they try again. They step back, waiting. Nothing happens for the longest while. They have thoughts that maybe, just maybe, there is nobody on the other side of it.

But then the gate opens, slowly. It's a heavy gate. Four guards are around them immediately, wanting to know who they are, and what business they have with the Blood Baron.

CHAPTER 12

THE SUN SETS COMPLETELY when they arrive at the gate to the expansive compound. The time has come for Noah to do what he's been dreading all along. After a brief conversation with the guards at the gate, they are let in. Sophia's stomach is turning.

They are escorted through a maze that leads up to the main house. It's everything but how they pictured it. Sophia's home was more tyrannical than this. It is beautiful!

Neatly trimmed hedges form a labyrinth from the gate, making you feel like you've just entered a wonderland. As they make their way up on horseback towards the house, they both forget the reason that they are actually here. Noah wonders how four hundred horses fitted in the labyrinth until he sees a field to either side of the maze that could house a thousand.

Coming up on the house is no less impressive. It's a grand structure, architects probably from France or Italy. You can just about make out the massive staircase in the entrance hall through glass panels that serve as part of the front door. For all intents and purposes, it is a very modern structure, the likes of which neither Noah nor Sophia have seen before, not even at any of the castles Sophia visited in her former life.

"It's new," is all the guard manages to give them by way of explanation for this grand structure.

"It's magnificent," is what Sophia manages before she remembers why she is here.

She pauses at the bottom of the stairs leading to the impressive front door, knowing that once she crosses over, once she is on the other side, she will never be able to go back. Sophia holds her belly, knowing too what this means for her baby. She will have to play it as well as she can. Noah can never know, not now, not ever!

They've been expected for a while now, the servants who fuss over her making this obvious. "We thought you would never get here little miss," a polite older woman named Hagar. She is every bit like the grandmother Sophia remembers, hers but not quite.

"We had some trouble along the way, but I'm here now." Sophia is trying to be brave, for her own sake as well as her family's. She knows she's late. But better late than never, right.

Noah is shown a room where he can prepare himself. He looks a sight, and so does Sophia. She is taken away by Hagar and some other attendants to prepare her for presentation. After all, she can't be presented to her husband-to-be in the state that she is in. Everyone is excited by the arrival. They are relieved actually, knowing that this will soften their boss somewhat, hopefully!

After two hours she is ready. A dress that looks and feels like it was made for her on; bathed; light blusher on her face. Nothing else is needed. She is a vision, truly beautiful. Sophia wonders if this fairytale will end when she meets the Blood Baron. She remembers reading somewhere how really evil people like to surround themselves with nice things. So she doesn't let herself assume that he will be as nice as everything or everyone so far.

They find him in the dining room. He stands up as they enter, motioning for Sophia to sit, Noah too. They do, taken aback by how fragile this monster looks. He looks like a man defeated, but nobody says anything. Instead, Noah stands again and introduces Sophia properly.

"There's a matter for us to discuss in private," he says, referring to the letter, the contract that the Blood Baron needs to sign. He suddenly feels like he could take him, there and then, a knife from the table through his heart. But he doesn't, sitting down instead to a very elaborate dinner.

Sophia says very little throughout dinner, answering only the questions that she is asked. She doesn't even speak to Noah, who is having difficulty with conversation. The Baron speaks easily, not even mentioning that they should have been here weeks ago. He just seems relieved that Sophia is here, that she has been presented to him, and that he can marry her as soon as possible. He dispatches a messenger to ride hard and catch up with the army, to tell them that the raid is not necessary.

He is running out of time, his energy leaving him. So he will have to make her his wife soon so as to consummate their relationship. And hopefully, this consummation will lead to an heir. That is after all what this is about. What it's always been about!

After dinner he lets the pair go. Rooms have been prepared for them. He will sign the contract tomorrow. For now, he will sleep peacefully, more so than he has done in a very long time.

"Dream of our wedding my dear, and let me know

tomorrow what it is you would like." This is how he bids Sophia goodnight. Both she and Noah are asleep as soon as their heads hit the pillows, sheer exhaustion.

The house is abuzz with wedding preparations by the time Sophia wakes. She is served breakfast in bed, with everyone excitedly telling her what's going on. It is well after ten but nobody cares. She's had a hard journey and if she wants to sleep in a bit then so be it. Sophia remembers her belly. She rubs it, thinking that maybe, just maybe, the little one will be happy here. She could be happy too, if she tried, she reassures herself.

Hagar comes in after her bath. She needs to measure for her wedding dress. This sends home for Sophia that Noah will soon leave her here alone amongst these strangers. That soon she will be married to a man she doesn't know or love. Sophia finally breaks down, sobbing uncontrollably. Hagar has a reassuring hand on her shoulder, the others in the room looking on not knowing what to do.

"He's not that bad love, once you get used to him." Hagar is anything but reassuring and Sophia continues to cry.

She cries for everything that she has left behind. She cries because of the perilous journey she undertook to get here. She cries mostly for Noah. She has never felt for anyone what she feels for him. And now he will be leaving her here, married to another man who will raise their child as his own. She cries eventually just for the sake of crying and then stops.

Sophia pulls herself together, just enough for Hagar to do what she came in to do. Hagar measures her under her arms, then her length. Then she measures her belly, lingering just long enough in the area for Sophia to know that she knows. Everybody else is too excited about the upcoming wedding to notice. But Hagar's experience is such that she notices this immediately.

"Leave us." She orders the others out of the room. They look confused but eventually get the message and leave. "How long has it been my dear?" Hagar asks, assuming correctly that Sophia knows that she is pregnant.

"How do you know, it can't be more than a few weeks?" Sophia is astonished that Hagar would know this from merely feeling her belly.

"My dear, I've seen my share of children born, and their mothers too. Trust me, I know." Suddenly Hagar is her confidante, the knower of her secret. What she will do with this information is unclear, but Sophia knows after she tells her the story she will understand. She just has to.

Hagar does understand. But this just means that Sophia will have to get herself into the Baron's bed quickly so that no one will be any wiser. She appreciates Hagar in that moment, but she misses her mother more. This is something that she should have liked to have shared with her mother. But she is a woman now. And a woman has a duty to her house. This is Sophia's house now!

Meanwhile Noah, anxious, stands before the tyrant. The contract is in his hands, albeit a little messed up. The journey has taken its toll on the little piece of paper as well. Noah just wants it signed so he can leave. He will never make peace with the fact that he left Sophia here. But what can he do? He may as well just get it over and done with. Looking around him, he knows that Sophia will eventually be happy here. He hopes as much anyway.

Noah shifts his weight from foot to foot, the Blood Baron looking almost through him. He wonders what this is about. Why the stares? The older man seems to want to ask

Noah something that he cannot. Noah wonders what this is, handing over the contract.

"You know, this isn't how I expected it to be." The same tone as last night, the Blood Baron is as calm and collected.

"What, your marriage?" Noah is careful with his response.

"No, my life!" The sudden openness throws Noah and he doesn't know what to say.

He proceeds to tell Noah of his escapades. He regales him with tales of his conquests, as though they were all above board. For an hour the Blood Baron goes on an on about how he annihilated entire villages, plundering and pillaging everything and everyone.

The Baron pauses briefly and looks at Noah. He seems to see right through him and not all at the same time. Something about Noah's appearance seems to trouble him. It seems to intrigue him as well. But he does not say what.

"I think it's best if you stay for another day or two, just to rest up before making the journey back," more an order than a suggestion. Noah doesn't know how to respond, except to look at the contract, still unsigned, in the Blood Baron's hands. He nods, knowing that he needs the rest, but also wanting to get back to his life, without Sophia.

"There's just something about him," is all the Blood Baron can manage. He is surrounded by his council, a group of wise men and one woman, who advise him on matters pertaining to his estate. He says it over and over again. Even when asked about Sophia he brushes it off, making them think that at least for the moment, she were less important.

And she is. He has her now. She is going nowhere, set to marry him shortly and then give him a string of sons. Or just one. One would do, just to make sure that his entire estate doesn't fall into the hands of his staff. Not that he doesn't trust them or that he won't leave them with anything. But the legacy, his legacy, is far more important to him. It's too important to be left to servants.

He lets Noah go without signing the contract, saying that he will get to it later. For now Noah must explore the expansive grounds, and the house, keeping himself busy until the Blood Baron signs. Noah doesn't know why the delay and he hates it. But at least he seems unlikely to see Sophia between now and the time he leaves.

The Blood Baron is in council for most of the day, convinced that Noah is his long-lost son. The members of his council are somewhat convinced, but not sure. They need to be sure. And how will Noah respond to the news? Will he be accepting of this tyrant as his father, although the Blood Baron seems to have softened over the last while? Or maybe it is just his way, a silent assassin. Maybe he is just as calm on the battlefield, calm yet totally ruthless. This is what Noah wonders as he walks through the house, how someone so gentle, so soft, could have the reputation that the Blood Baron has. How someone so nice could have done all the things he himself admitted to doing when he told Noah tales of all his escapades!

There is one way for them to be sure, but they need to keep Noah around to find out. Noah's birthmark will be the confirmation that they need. But they will need to see it. How though, since they can't just undress him to see. Well, they can, but this will be too much. And the last thing the Blood Baron wants now is to upset Noah, especially since he may be his long-lost son. He may not be though, but the Baron is sure that he is. He just has to be!

His eyes are his mother's. His complexion is hers as well. This is what has sparked the Baron's interest. How a young man could so closely resemble the love the Baron lost all those years ago, when he was really ruthless, truly evil, is uncanny. He just has to know!

He invites Noah to stay for the feast that will mark his wedding. Noah doesn't want to; not wanting to see Sophia married to another man. He just wants to be gone from this place, now that he knows that she will be treated fairly at least. He knows that she will at least be treated with care, if not by the Blood Baron, then by his staff. He has no idea that Sophia is pregnant with his child.

A young page is given to Noah, to help him with various things like getting dressed while he is in the Blood Baron's house. Noah finds this strange and a little unacceptable given his position in the house where he comes from. Rowan had always treated him fairly but he never treated him like this, like he was royalty.

Noah finds it all very strange. But soon enough he is comfortable enough with the arrangement to let the young page help him dress. And this is just the gap that the Blood Baron needed, just what he had hoped for. Putting his shirt on, the page is very excited, but can't say why. He helps Noah get ready urgently, almost too enthusiastically now. Then he leaves to inform the Blood Baron about the birth-mark he has seen with his own two eyes.

"I knew it, I knew it!" The Blood Baron is very excited now. His excitement is clouded with just a little bit of nervous tension. He knows now that Noah is definitely his long-lost son. He is certain about it. Still. He needs to be sure.

Three days pass, and he has no idea how to be sure. He eats alone, Noah and Sophia also eating separately. He meets with his counselors every day for the three days, trying to come up with a way to be sure. He could just ask him of his history, but Noah was so young when he and his mother fled that his mother could have told him anything about his father's whereabouts. He might even have been raised by another man, a man who proved to be more of a father to Noah than he could have been at the time. It's all very perplexing for the Baron. And in his current state, the strain is starting to show.

He meets with Sophia to discuss their wedding preparations. But he is distracted. Sophia notices this and asks him about it, trying to sound as enthusiastic as she can about the wedding. After all, her stomach might just start showing soon, and she needs to be married by then. She will explain the issue of her virginity if it ever comes up. But somehow she knows that a man of the Baron's age won't really be concerned that she is no longer a virgin; just as long as she gives him a son.

Sophia also has no idea that Noah is still in the house. She is kept on one side of it, where preparations can happen without her being involved in the Blood Baron's life. Not yet, anyway. Noah is kept on the opposite side of the house, near the Blood Baron's bedroom. To be so close to his son is almost too much for the old man. But he needs to play it well, just in case Noah isn't his son. Everyone agrees, however, that Noah is!

The Baron decides that he needs to know for sure. He calls for Noah and his counselors. There is no time like the present to make sure, and the only way to be sure is to interrogate the source. They have decided to interrogate Noah.

"You've got your mother's eyes boy!" The Blood Baron cannot hold himself back any longer. They've been skirting the issue at hand, enquiring everything about Noah that just keeps confirming what the old man knows in his heart. Noah was barely three years old when he was taken from the house, this very house that he is in awe of. It was a tough decision for his mother, but she did what she thought was best for the boy at the time. And it was, otherwise the Blood Baron would have turned him into a carbon copy of the man he was at the time.

"Excuse me," Noah manages after clearing his throat.

Noah doesn't resemble his father in any way, except for his birthmark. So the interrogation and subsequent reference to his mother don't make any sense to him. Even when the old man excuses his council and proceeds to weep bitterly on Noah's shoulder, it doesn't register with him. He finds it all strange and bewildering.

"I am your father boy, your father," the Blood Baron says while removing the clothing covering his own birthmark, revealing the wound at the same time. Noah lifts his shirt and just stares at the intricate markings. He gazes at the Baron's birthmark for a long time, not sure what this means. He remembers the stories his mother told him about who his father was, and for a moment doesn't believe this man. But the birthmarks are a copy of each other, and this could mean just one thing.

Noah doesn't know how to respond to this. He just lets the old man cry on his shoulder and then embraces him. They are alone in the room for the longest time, and even when the older man has stopped weeping, they just stand there looking at each other. This is the last thing Noah expected. He had given up hope of ever seeing his father, ever meeting him. And with all that he knew about him, he didn't want to.

But nowhere he was, a man broken. He was definitely not the man he'd heard so many stories about over the years, at least not anymore. He was still strong, yet fragile, vulnerable almost. And Noah cannot hold back from embracing him any longer. Noah pulls his father to him and hugs him fiercely. It is a tight grip, so tight that at any moment they might fall over. He lets him go before this happens though.

The Baron wants to know everything about Noah, about his life since leaving this house. He wants to know about the trials and tribulations that his son had to go through outside of the protection of his home. He wants to know about the hearts Noah has broken, or if he has married yet, or if he has his own children. But mostly he wants to know about his mother.

"Is she still alive?"

"Yes, and very happy!" Noah says this without thinking. But his mother had seemed happier as the years went on, and the memories faded.

"I don't blame her for taking you away. I would probably have done the same had I been in her position."

"She did what any mother would do." Noah feels the need to defend his mother now, despite the fact that the Baron is much changed. It is the son's duty to defend his mother regardless, even from his own father. Noah hugs the Baron again. Again it is long and intense. But then he remembers Sophia.

"I love her you know, the girl." He says this only after he has created sufficient distance between him and his father. He can't be sure how the Baron will respond to this proclamation of love for his soon-to-be wife.

"Who, Sophia?"

"Yes, Sophia!" Noah needs to say it. He needs to get it out before he loses his nerve, and Sophia, to his father. He looks him square in the face in anticipation of his response. Noah is nervous though, very nervous, unsure of just what this response might be.

They just stare at each other for the longest time. And then the Baron leaves the room. Noah is now anxious, not knowing what this means. He realizes that it could be bad for both him and Sophia. But just how bad he doesn't know.

After what feels like ages the Baron returns, Sophia in tow. He has the broadest grin on his face, and seems to have got a bit of the spring in his step back, although he still stands with some difficulty. He falls into a chair and bursts into the loudest laughter. Neither Noah nor Sophia knows what this means. But they can't stop looking at each other.

Sophia had no idea that Noah was even still in the house, and she can't hide her smile, even if it is just because she has had the chance to look upon him again. Noah smiles at her through his anxiety, the Baron still caught in the throws of his laugh. Eventually, he starts to gather himself, encouraging the two to sit.

They sit, looking from each other to the man who is even softer and kinder now. They cannot bring themselves to join in the laughter since they don't know what he is laughing at, or what it means. The pair keeps throwing their eyes at the door as if at any moment a battalion of henchmen might come barging through it to take them away. But then the Baron just looks at them, the grin on his face returned.

"So, the two of you are in love I take it or is it just my boy here who is smitten?" He asks this with the same laughter in his voice.

"Your boy?" Sophia is confused.

Noah begins to explain what has happened. The Baron chirps in every chance he gets, Noah not getting to the part where he is the Baron's son fast enough. Sophia is even more confused, not knowing what this means for her now. Again the Baron asks if they are in love, and this time Noah answers an emphatic yes. She manages a nod.

All preparations are halted. The news is too much for

Sophia so she has to lie down. Hagar takes her to her room, elated by the news. The house fills quickly with the return of the long-lost Noah and everyone breathes a collective sigh of relief. The appearance of an heir will go a long way in placating the Blood Baron they know.

Messengers are dispatched to Sophia's home to inform them of the news. She is with a child and will marry the father of the little one shortly. They are sure to mention that it is Noah and not the Baron. A special message is sent to Noah's mother as well. It is hoped that they will be here shortly so that they can marry Noah and Sophia as soon as possible. The Blood Baron, no longer a fitting name, is excited and nervous all at once.

He knows from Noah that his mother never remarried. He knows that she has been happier over the last while than she's ever been, but he hopes that this has something to do with the pain of losing him becoming less with the passage of time. He is hopeful, but not too hopeful, knowing that the man he once was, the man that earned the reputation of the Blood Baron, was not a man that could be easily missed. Still, he allows himself to dream of spending the last years of his life with the only woman he has ever loved.

It is six days before the carriages ferrying the guests of honor would arrive. And a further two hours before they have settled enough for Noah and Sophia to be called to greet them. The Baron has first to speak to Sophia's parents, to apologize, to welcome them into his family. Rowan and Mary take his apology and let it sit for a while in their heads before they accept it. Then they just want to see their daughter.

Mary grabs Sophia and holds her tightly to her as though she might at any moment disappear. Rowan stands a distance away, tentative. He isn't sure how she will receive him after what he had done to her.

"I'm sorry!" is all he can manage. This is the long and short of their conversation, with him repeating how sorry he was and she telling him that there was no need to apologize. All have turned out well for everyone after all. There is no need for sorries.

Noah and his mother are left in the parlor talking with the Baron. They stand apart, Noah watching his parents. He knows how his mother feels about his father, so he doesn't push her. It's all in the Baron's hands now.

They look at each other for the longest time, not saying anything. Their heads are filled with things to say but the words won't come out of their mouths. Then the Baron lets out a laugh, as raucous as the previous one, and the ice is broken. Noah's mother joins in the laughter, knowing exactly what they are saying to each other but not. This is all that is needed.

He takes her hand and looks at it for the longest while, his laugh now a giggle. He cannot believe how things have worked out. He cannot believe this second chance at a family that he has received. He definitely will not let it slip through his fingers.

The double wedding is beautiful. Sophia wears a white pastel gown with crystal detail, obviously from Paris. Her mother-in-law wears a lavender gown, also a pastel shade. The Baron and his son are dressed identically, their looks rounded off with magnificent white coattails. It is truly a spectacle.

There are bridesmaids and groomsmen. Sophia's mother is the maid of honor for both women, which goes against custom, but neither woman would have it any other way. Rowan walks them both down the aisle.

The garden has been transformed into even more of a wonderland than it already was. Lanterns are everywhere, in a soft shade of cream. They are lit come late afternoon and they pick up the colors of the flowers. The tables are laden with food, delicacies from London, confectionery, and pastries from the best in the business.

Walkways are lined with silk the same shade as the lanterns. They form mirrors to pick up the coloring around them. Weddings are a truly magnificent affair, one that will be spoken about for as long as it takes for there to be a better, more splendid affair.

The wedding tent is at the bottom of the garden. It is a wonderland of silks and other fabrics in rich bold colors. The Baron had intended for it to be for him and his young bride, but this is no longer necessary. He leads Noah and Sophia to it and lets them go inside. Nobody will disturb them until they come out of it to start their new lives together. Everyone is happy with the outcome, but no one is happier than Rowan. He looks out over the expansive grounds, content that he can return home with a clear heart and conscience. And confident that when his grandchild is born, they will once again be sent for to celebrate.

ABOUT THE AUTHOR

Johana Gardener is an emerging erotica author of many erotica kinks and sub-genres. Be sure to check out other books and leave a review if this story got you hot!

Visit my blog at Johana Gardener Blog

Join my newsletter for exclusive Johana Gardener Newsletter

Sign up for Free Stories from Xplicit Press Authors

Xplicit Press Author Updates

Like Xplicit Press on Facebook

Follow Xplicit Press on Twitter

Readers: I want to expand a few of the stories to see where the characters can be explored further. If there are any of the stories that you would like to read more about again, I'd love to hear from you!

Keep In Touch
Johana Gardener
info@johanagardener.com